JUST BECAUSE IT HAPPENED TO YOU DOESN'T MAKE IT INTERESTING

ISBN 978-1-7353286-8-3

Just Because It Happened to You Doesn't Make It Interesting

DWFC: N30/24/234

First Edition. Published December 2024

www.27bslash6.com

By the Same Author:

The Internet is a Playground
A *New York Times* bestselling book about overdue accounts, missing cats, and pie charts.

Look Evelyn, Duck Dynasty Wiper Blades, We Should Get Them
A book about design agencies, above ground pools, and magic tea.

That's Not How You Wash a Squirrel
A book about toasted sandwiches, sociopathy, and secret underground tunnels.

Wrap It In a Bit of Cheese Like You're Tricking the Dog
A book about suggestion boxes, buttons, and third-degree burns.

Walk It Off, Princess
A book about cantilevers, secret spots, and Antarctic expeditions.

Deadlines Don't Care if Janet Doesn't Like Her Photo
A book about fish people, office romance, and big red rocks.

Let's Eat Grandma's Pills
A travel book about frogs, buckets, and transparent bubble pods.

For Seb, Holly, and Chester

Not you, Banksy. Why are you barking? Also, big shout out
to my neighbours, Bald Guy and Nora, for all the remodelling
they've done this year. The circular saw is my favourite tool.
Also for choosing a contractor with Tourette's to do the work.
Almost every sentence in this book has been accompanied by
Shania Twain's *Man! I Feel Like A Woman!* played on loop
from a pickup truck while an old guy yells, "HUUH!"

Alternative Titles For This Book

Go-Karting Tips and Tricks

It's Okay to Fur Up a Bit in Winter

Samsung Dryer Tunes

These Are a Few of My Least Favourite Things

Gary's Teeth and Other Horror Stories

We Have Josh Gad at Home. It's a Pig

Poo Bags

What's the Actual Point of a Kazoo?

Bag Sealing - A Guide

Filling Voids With Copier Paper

Whose Sand is This?

Knifespawn 5: The Golden Hat

Bat Wing Sleeves

Lynn Hurst is a Bit of a Dickhead

Thin

Contents

Introduction i

Free Eggs 1

Distractions 21

And Then the Robots Attacked 39

Sleep 47

Turtle 52

Turtles 53

Who Knew Go-Karting Was So Dangerous? 57

Mystery Monday 85

A Black Man Riding a Bike 98

Do We Get Prep Time? 99

Too Many Turtles 105

That Pumpkin 112

Interpersonal Conflict Resolution 113

Writer's Block 116

Friday's Intellectual Office Discourse 117

The Vibrating Man 135

About the Author 193

Introduction

I flew to Atlanta with my coworker Walter recently. We didn't see any peaches, but we did see a homeless lady pooing in a KFC bucket. It was a short trip, just for the day, to look at a retail space our agency is designing the graphics for. The space looked exactly how it looked in the photos, so I'm not sure what the point of flying there to see the space in person was. Walter measured a couple of walls while I pretended to take notes, then we caught an Uber back to the airport.

That's how most of our trips are at the moment. We picked up a few new clients in different states this year, which necessitates travel, but the clients aren't large enough to justify *enjoyable* travel. Walter still enjoys the flying part though, which is why I take him, his wonder at seeing the world from cloud-height hasn't diminished since his first flight two years ago. It's like having a puppy on the plane, something fun and frisky to distract you from the fact you're flying to Alabama.

"Boo. It's just farmland. No, wait, there's a pond. It's not very big though. We should fly somewhere with mountains. There's no mountains here. Have you ever flown over a mountain?"

"Yes, Holly and I have flown over the Rockies a few times on our way to Seattle. We also flew over Mount Ranier, the active volcano once."

"When it was going?"

"When what was going?"

"The volcano."

"Yes, the plane had to do a barrel roll to avoid a large plume of magma."

"Press x to doubt."

"Sorry?"

"It's a meme."

"Is it?"

"Yes, it's from a video game."

"Okay."

"It works better as a picture."

At one point during the flight, Walter mentioned he had read one of my books. It was surprising, as he has stated on several occasions he doesn't read. When I relayed my surprise, he stated, "Proper books. I don't read proper books. With proper stories. Yours was just stupid stuff about buckets. I liked the story about me though."

Apparently Walter and Ashley - his girlfriend who also works at the agency - stayed with Ashley's parents for two days, and there was no technology because Ashley's parents are Amish.

"You stayed in an Amish community?"
"No, we stayed at the beach."
"What? Are you sure Ashley's parent's are Amish? She's never mentioned it."
"They didn't have the Internet. They didn't even have a television."
"That doesn't make them Amish. Did they drive a horse and buggy?"
"No. They have a Subaru Forester."
"Right, so I'm guessing there wasn't a lot of barn building going on at the beach."
"No, nothing was going on. We just sat around doing nothing. How long do you reckon it would take you to get bored sitting on a deck looking at the ocean?"
"Are drugs involved?"
"No."
"Maybe thirty minutes."
"Exactly. That's why I read your book."
"Ashley's parent's had a copy of my book?"
"No, Ashley had it on her Kindle. Her parents just have proper books. Mostly military stuff, her dad was in the Army."

I knew immediately which book Walter was referring to. I've mentioned Walter in a couple of my books but there's only one about buckets. The story Walter was referring to wasn't *about him* though, it was about a work trip to Asheville. Sure, he was *in* the story, but that's like saying *The Very Hungry Caterpillar* is about fruit.

"So you're saying I'm fruit?"

"No, I'm saying the story wasn't just about you."

"Well, I was in it and it was the best story. The rest were just kind of 'yeah and this happened'."

"Yeah and this happened?"

"Yeah, and then other stuff. Just because it happened to you doesn't make it interesting."

"Wow."

"No offence, but if you want to sell more books, you should write about something more interesting than buckets. Like really deep caves that have blind fish living in them."

"Or more stories about you."

"Exactly."

There are definitely more stories 'about Walter' in this book than my other titles. It's why he's in this introduction. He's not as interesting as cave fish, but hopefully his assessment of what readers want has some merit as most of this book is about the agency and the people I work with. Not all of it of course, there's also some stuff about sleeping, go-karts, and watching television... Maybe I'll go spelunking between now and my next book and see some blind fish to write about, but I haven't done anything exciting this year. It's been a year, not an interesting year, just a year. That's how years are sometimes; you work, you watch television, you buy a mattress. Not every year can be a blind fish year.

We did lose an employee this year. Not in the traditional sense of them quitting or dying, but we don't know where Rebecca, our production manager, is. Earlier this year, she stated she was going to "work remotely for a bit" and never came back. She had some stuff going on in her life, but that's no reason not to clearly state, "I discovered my husband prefers the company of men, so I emptied our bank account, bought an RV, and plan to drive across America. It won't affect my work."

The first we learned of Rebecca's RV adventure is when she joined a Zoom call from the Niagara Falls visitor center parking lot. Every Zoom call since has been from a parking lot. Most of them have been Walmart parking lots though.

It actually hasn't affected Rebecca's work in the slightest. If anything, she's more responsive. The only difference is that we can't walk into her office to lie about why projects aren't completed, we have to email her the lies, which means she has everything in writing so we have to check what lies we emailed her before emailing new lies to ensure the lies don't conflict.

"Rebecca's asking about the deodorant label, Ben."
"Tell her I have Covid."
"Hmm... you've already had Covid twice this month. I'll tell her you have scabies."
"What's scabies?"
"It's similar to shingles."
"That works."

Ben, our copy writer, has a new girlfriend. His last girlfriend broke up with him because he took photos of her sleeping. His new girlfriend isn't much to look at it, but she makes up for it in personalities. She has around fourteen. One is a surly mechanic named Jim. None of them use soap. Apparently they met on a Warhammer 40K server, but I don't know what that is so I don't have a joke for it. Ben attempted to explain it once, but I wasn't paying attention because he had a little moth in his beard.

We also gained a new employee this year, but she was only here for three days. Having worked with our creative director Mike for so long, I sometimes forget how he can come across. It's not that he's intentionally cruel, he's just incapable of withholding a remark if he thinks it's clever.

"First day?"
"Yes."
"And that's what you decided to wear?"
"You don't like my overalls?"
"You look like you're about to trick Huckleberry Finn into painting your fence."
"That wasn't Huckleberry Finn. It was a boy named Ben. Have you even read the book?"
"Wow, you're not going last long around here with that attitude."

I should also mention that Mike's husband, Patrick, joined a community theatre group at the start of this year. It's the same theatre group that Jodie, our senior designer, was once a member of. Jodie invited Patrick to join and within a few weeks, Patrick took over and kicked her out. It was like the show *Succession* here for a while. At one point, Patrick came to the agency and put up a flyer for a play in the front window, and Jodie tore it down. Patrick put up another, because he had 500 copies, and he and Jodie did the 'it's duck season, no it's rabbit season' thing for about five minutes until Mike told Patrick he wasn't allowed to put up a flyer in the window because this isn't a Goodwill store. It turned into a whole thing about Mike not being supportive of his acting career and taking Jodie's side. It was a betrayal of his trust and he wasn't sure he could continue in the relationship. It was essentially domestic violence and he'd have to live in a shelter.

I'm kind of with Patrick on this. We all just want someone who chooses us over everyone else under any circumstance. Even if the circumstance is stupid.

Patrick did move out for a few days - he stayed at a Hilton, not a shelter - but he missed his space toilet too much. It's from Japan and cost twelve-thousand dollars. It looks like a cryogenic pod and heats, massages, cleans and dries while playing rainforest sounds. After you've finished, it sends a message to your phone with a stool analysis. It's nice, but I don't need my toilet to tell me to drink more water and twelve grand seems a lot to listen to frogs while having your bum blow-dried. Having tried it out though, the next time I used my toilet at home, it was kind of like I was living in the 1700s.

Their whole house is like that; I avoid going there because it just makes me feel bad about how I live.

"Why do we live like this, Holly?"
"Like what?"
"Like paupers. We don't even have a refrigerator with a big television screen on the front that shows what's inside when you tap it."

That's the point of having nice things though, I guess. To make people jelly. We don't have anything nice at our house, we just have dogs.

I'm treating this intro as both a 'year in review' and a 'cast of characters' but I'm not going to write anything about Kate, our HR director. Mainly because I've been instructed not to. Some people are all friendly and easy-going until you write about them kayaking with their black friend. Note that I wrote 'some people', not anyone specific. I fully understand writing about a coworker's personal life fosters an environment of distrust.

We just learned Melissa, our front desk human, is pregnant again. She, and her husband Scoutmaster Andrew, are hoping for a baby with a normal shaped head this time. They haven't stated that, but that's my guess. Their first baby's head was shaped like an avocado when it was new, but it looks more like a gourd now. They make it wear one of those headband things with a little bow on it to try to disguise the shape, but it just draws attention to it. A hat isn't any better, it looks like there's an apple hidden under it. Melissa also received a pay increase this year; child care is expensive and Mike doesn't want the baby at the agency. He claims it's because Melissa changed a diaper on the boardroom table, but we've had private discussions about the shape of the baby's head and he doesn't like looking at it either.

"I mean, how does it look to clients? They walk in expecting to be greeted professionally and instead there's a mutant baby staring at them."
"Mutant is a bit much. It's head is just gourd shaped."
"What shaped?"
"Gourd shaped."
"What the fuck is a gourd?"
"It's a type of squash."
"Then why didn't you just say squash?"
"Fine, it's squash shaped."
"No, it's more like those things bible people drank out of. They also make bird houses out of them."
"Gourds."
"No, it's some kind of dried pumpkin."

Who haven't I mentioned? Oh, Gary of course. And Jason. Jason doesn't get a mention, he never does, because he wants one too badly. I've written several books while I've been at the agency and Scoutmaster Andrew has had more mentions than Jason. All you need to know about Jason is that he wears blue shirts with a white collar. I know, right? It's not 1996 and he's not a loan officer at a bank. Scoutmaster Andrew has better fashion sense and he wears a lot of Carhartt. Jason and Scoutmaster Andrew don't get along very well. Jason claims it's because he once went on a date with Melissa - they went to the cinema to see *Captain America: The Winter Soldier* - but everyone knows it's a jealousy thing; Scoutmaster Andrew has hiker's thighs and a dashing smile, while Jason has Swiffer handle legs and periodontal disease. Really, I'm the victim in all this as I have to throw away a lot of content just to avoid mentioning Jason. The above doesn't count because it was more about Scoutmaster Andrew than Jason.

It's been a big year for Gary though, he's had about fourteen medical emergencies and two near-death experiences. He almost drowned in a very slippery bathtub, and a wasp stung him on the neck while he was passing a truck on a highway. Both are terrible ways to almost die. Apparently Gary and his wife stayed at a resort called The Omni Homestead for their 45th wedding anniversary, and the oversized Victorian claw tub in their suite was too Pledged. Gary only had one working hand at the time because a client had slammed his other one in a van door a few weeks prior. I was with Gary when it happened - the hand incident, not in the bath with him - and I still hear his scream sometimes. It was like a Magic Bullet blender on full speed mixed with a goat bleat. He broke three fingers and two tips were cut off. They were more squished off actually, one the tips was still hanging on by a bit of skin. I had to drive him to the hospital in his 1993 Saab 900, so again I was the victim in all this.

Gary has a different car now; he rolled the Saab over an embankment after being stung. Surprisingly, he wasn't hurt apart from a few bruises and a welt, but the car was a write-off. He replaced it with a 1998 Jaguar XJ8 so I don't know what's wrong with him. I've only been in it once and the dash fell out when I tried to open the glovebox. I'm not sure what it is with old guys and old cars. Maybe it's a camaraderie thing along the lines of, "Yes, you're past your prime but you're still handsome and very much desired. You're actually much better than the younger models, they don't have cassette players."

It's not just old guys of course, I know a guy in his mid-thirties named Michael who is into classic cars. There's nothing in this book about Michael, but mentioning him gives me an excuse to include the following photo of him. I didn't take the photo, I saved it to my phone off Facebook a few years ago, and the only reason I have it is because of his shorts. Who wears shorts this large? It's like someone stitched two windsocks together. Either his thighs are gas cylinder sized or there's a lot of air circulation happening. Probably a lot of swishing as well.

"What's in your pocket, Michael?"
"Two watermelons and a 42-piece screwdriver set."
"No, your other pocket."
"Oh, that's my grandma. She's baking."

In addition to Gary's fingers, the Pledged tub, and the embankment flip, he's had far too many minor accidents to list them all - so here's my top five:

1. A raccoon scared him when he went outside to put a kitchen tidy bag in the trash and he pulled a muscle in his neck. It was pretty severe; his head was locked to the left and up, like he was looking at something in a tree. He had to do neck exercises with a tennis ball for three weeks.

2. He drank water out of a garden hose then spent four days in hospital.

3. Walter shot a Nerf gun dart at Gary, and Gary headbutted a door frame attempting to dodge it. Over the next few days, a small bump on his forehead grew to the size of a lemon and he had to get it lanced due it stretching the skin so much he couldn't close his right eye. Also, we all had to watch an OHS video about a guy named Reckless Ricky who works on a construction site.

4. He cracked a walnut and a fragment of shell flew into his eye. It doesn't matter how many times in your life you're told not to rub it, you always rub it. They had to remove it from his cornea with a robot arm.

And **5.** my personal favourite, Gary fell over a short fence at a petting zoo and a pig bit his shoulder.

I was originally going to make this a top ten, but most of Gary's incidents were kind of disappointing after the pig bite.

"I won't be in today."
"OH MY GOD WHAT HAPPENED?"
"I burned my stomach on a waffle maker."
"Oh, is that all?"
"It's a pretty bad burn."
"Well that's something I suppose. Is it at least in the shape of a waffle? Like does it have the pattern?"
"No, it's just a line."

I've managed to avoid any medical mishaps this year. I did have an annoying piece of corn stuck between my teeth for about a week and I punched myself in the face while pulling a cork out of a wine bottle, but nothing that required time off work. I had to make up reasons for not being at work and there's only so many times you can have a flat tire or put down your dog. I read somewhere that if you get a flat tire you should take a photo to use it again as an excuse in the future, which might also work with a dead dog, but I haven't had any flat tires or dead dogs this year.

I can't use the dead dog excuse at work anyway; Holly posts several photos a day of our dogs and she's friends with Kate on Facebook. It would be a lot easier if we had ten dogs that all look the same, that way I could have a rotation system. Names that sound the same would also help, like Robby, Bobby, and Knobby. A boring breed nobody gives a fuck about, like Labradors or Golden Retrievers, would work best. Our dogs are too ugly to be unmemorable.

"I won't be in today, we're putting down our dog."
"Which one? The insane Dalmatian/goat mix that bites kids or the retarded Boston terrier that always has something hanging out of its anus?"

Mostly I just don't turn up and hope nobody notices. My door is usually closed and nobody's declaring, "Where's David? His sunny disposition is required." I still have to meet client deadlines, but having worked in the design industry for so many years, I've established a five-stage process for that:

1. I have ages to do it.

2. I still have ages to do it.

3. I should build a greenhouse. That way we could grow our own tomatoes year-round.

4. I should probably come up with an excuse for why I haven't started yet. Maybe invent a relative with pancreatic cancer or claim I was kidnapped.

5. Coffee and cigarettes.

Stage 3 can be any activity requiring a credit card and several weeks of labor. Once, when I had two days to design a 64-page annual report, I built a flying fox.

Also, the restrictions on repeating excuses to work colleagues doesn't apply to clients. After thirty years of coming up with reasons for project delays, there's zero shame left and practically every dire scenario has been covered. I've had at least forty dogs put down, an auntie die in a tractor accident, a nephew get washed off rocks while fishing, and my offspring, Seb, losing his sight after being spat at by a snake. I don't even care if the excuses are believable at this point, what are they going to do about it?

"Your wife is having emergency surgery for brain swelling after being hit on the head by a coconut?"
"Yes, it's far more common than people think."
"It is?"
"It's more common than moose attacks."
"I didn't even know Virginia has coconut trees."
"It was a washed up coconut. Someone threw it."

The only difference between client deadlines and book deadlines is that you have nobody to make excuses to apart from yourself, so step 4 is replaced with a semi-self-delusional reward system:

"How much have we written today, David?
"Seven lines about coconuts."
"Good job. You should take a break - maybe research chicken coop construction for the next six hours."
"That's an excellent idea, David."
"It's basically free eggs."

Free Eggs

I knew a guy in Australia, named Glen, who built his own chicken coop. You don't have to worry about insulation, wiring, or heating in Australia, you just steal a couple of chickens and a roll of wire from a Greek man's backyard. Every Greek man in Australia has chickens and rolls of wire in their backyard, it's just a thing. They also have a concrete fountain in their front yard that's never turned on, and three fat daughters.

Glen's chicken coop was basically a bed frame on cinder blocks with a tarp draped over the top. It looked like a homeless person's shelter, but chickens don't care about aesthetics. Glen's HOA did though; there were rules about eyesores and having chickens - unless you're Greek apparently - and Glen was given seven days to remove the coop.

Glen had become very attached to the chickens - they had names and personalities by then - and he decided that if the HOA understood how unique and special each chicken was, they would surely bend the rules.

It's possible Glen may have been autistic now that I think about it. He owned a lot of DVD collector box sets and that's usually a giveaway. It detracts from my point, but not overly, as he didn't have full-blown autism - like he wasn't a screamer or really good at Sodoku.

Seven days isn't long, unless your holding your breath or waiting for an Amazon package, but Glen managed to create a ten-page dossier for each chicken in that time. The typeface was large and a lot of it was bullet points, but that's still impressive. Each spiral-bound document included a photo of the chicken, character traits, likes and dislikes, and hopes for the future. There were eight chickens.

I had a quick flick through a couple of the dossiers and, while I don't recall the exact wording, they contained stuff like, "Bernadette strides around like a catwalk model, she's popular among the other chickens and doesn't she know it. Her favourite foods are pizza crusts, broccoli, and crickets. When she's not striding or eating, Bernadette enjoys looking at trees."

I'm not exaggerating, there were paragraphs about their favourite music, temperature preferences, and the kind of job each chicken would have if it were a human. One of them, I think it was Cathy, taught sign language to deaf kids.

If I'd been the person who received the chicken dossiers, I would have said, "Wow, this guy really loves his chickens. Fuck it, he can keep them." Partly out of sympathy, but more out of the fear that anyone capable of writing eighty pages about chickens in seven days could also be capable of turning up at the next HOA meeting armed. A mother hen will fight a hawk to protect her babies.

The person who did receive the chicken dossiers didn't think the same way however. Or maybe they did but were overruled by the president of the HOA - a stickler for the rules and jaded by a loveless marriage. We'll call him Carl as most HOA presidents are named either Carl or Doug. Occasionally there will be a Geoff or, heaven forbid, a Jan. I had a Jan in Australia once and she fined me for using an LED bulb in my porch light. The fuck do I care if everyone else's light is a soft yellow? I'm saving eight cents a month. There were definitely more moths though, she was right about that.

I don't know anything about the inner workings of a HOA, or how you become the president of one, but I assume it's similar to a dictatorship where you assume control, assassinate any opposing candidates, and distribute the wealth among yourself and other high-ranking HOA officials. I mean, who gets the money from fines? It doesn't go back into the neighborhood; nobody's declaring, "It's been a prosperous month, let's buy every resident a concrete bird bath for their yard."

If I were the president of a HOA, the only rule I'd have about chickens would be "Chickens? Sure. Don't go mad though. Like 400 chickens is way too many."

Don't feel sad for Glen, he was actually a bit of a dick. I lent him money once, to fund a lawnmowing service startup, and built him a nice website, but after mowing just two lawns, Glen decided it was too much work and said I could have the lawnmower.

Firstly, if I wanted a lawnmower, I would have bought one myself, a nicer one. Secondly, I lived on the fifth floor of an apartment building. He actually took the mower up in the elevator and left it outside my door.

I was pretty annoyed about the whole thing and changed Glen's website to a Photoshopped image of Glen having sex with a chicken. Glen then threatened to have his uncle, who ran a Karate dojo, break my arms because he owed Glen a favour for all the free eggs. Obviously this was after the chicken thing.

Also, Glen wasn't forced to give up his chickens immediately. There was a bit of back and forth over three months after he discovered a loophole in the HOA agreement.

While the rules regarding chicken coops were clearly defined, rules about what constitutes a 'household pet' were vague and open to interpretation, so Glen just moved the chickens inside.

There was a point in human history where it was common for people to keep livestock inside their homes. Back then people probably smelled as bad as the animals and a bit of pig poo in your soup added flavour, but eventually science was invented and someone suggested the animal thing could be contributing to the fact that seven out of ten children died before the age of five and nobody lived past thirty.

"Right, well I have a scratch on my leg. Guess that's it. It's been a good life and I've seen many things in my nineteen years. Remember that turnip shaped like a baby? Such fun."

I visited Glen's house just a few weeks after the chickens had been living inside, and for the next year or so, even seeing a picture of a chicken made me nauseated. I'm hesitant to attempt to describe the smell, but it was a bit like forgotten onions at the back of a cupboard that have started to liquify.

Even that doesn't describe the smell accurately. It's probably easier to just make a quick list of smells that are less offensive:

1. Cheese-clogged wet kitchen sponges that have been hiding under plates in a sink for a week.

2. A neighbour dying and decomposing over three weeks in the apartment next to yours.

3. My coworker Gary.

I'm not sure what it is with Gary, but you know the term 'old person smell'? Gary could be the poster child. I think it's partly because once you reach a certain age, a quick shake after urinating isn't the end of the process and your penis waits to be put away then says, "Hang on, here's a little bit more." Also, your sense of smell fades with age, so even if you give your trousers a quick sniff when you're getting dressed and think, "These are good for another few wears" they're probably not.

Gary's smell doesn't bother me too much. I just keep a can of air freshener on my desk and spray it at him whenever he approaches. I also placed several of those car air fresheners shaped like pine trees throughout his office, but he took them down and I had to have a meeting with Kate, our HR director. I explained it was a safety issue, as exposure to high concentrations of ammonia can cause burning of the nose, throat and respiratory tract, often leading to bronchiolar and alveolar edema, but I had to apologise to Gary and promise to stop spraying him. There's no rule against pulling my shirt up over my nose whenever he's close though.

Also, I did have a neighbour in the apartment next to me die and decompose over three weeks. I just thought he was cooking weird meals as he was Albanian. When health services eventually entered his premises, they discovered the note I had slipped under his door asking him to please use the vent when he cooks.

"And when did you first notice the smell?"

"A couple of weeks back."

"And you didn't think to notify someone?"

"I didn't want anyone to think I'm racist."

"The note says, "I don't know what weird Albanian shit you're cooking in there, but please use the vent. It smells like a decomposing pig in the corridor.""

"It did."

"That's kind of racist."

"Only because I wrote the word Albanian. Without it, it's fine."

"And what made you think he was Albanian?"

"I don't know, he just looked a bit rapey."

That was a joke. I don't think Albanians look rapey and I don't need you to email me letting me know you found the joke offensive because you're an Albanian who hasn't raped anyone in ages.

I know a guy named Raf who is Albanian and I asked him if he found the paragraph offensive. He did, but the fact that I know an Albanian completely offsets the whole racist thing. That's just how it works. You can say anything about anyone if you know one of them.

I also know a Rwandan guy. Not well, we're not friends, but I've seen him at the supermarket.

I didn't visit Glen's house again. I couldn't. I'd barely made it out. It was like those videos you see of soldiers in a hut having their eyes sprayed with pepper. You know the ones, sometimes the soldiers aren't in a hut, sometimes they have to pick up a tire and put it over a pole or something equally as stupid after being sprayed. There's probably a point to it, but if someone said to me, "Okay, we're going to need you to sit in this hut while we pepper spray you and then we want you to put a tire over a pole," I'd steal a Jeep and make a run for it.

Whenever I did bump into Glen, at social events and once on a jetty, he looked like he'd been swimming with his eyes open in a heavily over-chlorinated pool. His skin was a blotchy pink and his eyes were red. Not 'slightly bloodshot' red, more 'fast zombie' red.

I should probably expand on the jetty thing. It's one of those occasions I think about a couple of times a year, usually when I see a photo of a jetty or I'm watching one of those HGTV shows where couples look at beach properties to buy. It's not always couples of course, sometimes it's a guy and his mom and you think, 'A bit of a back-story on this relationship wouldn't go astray,' but you never get one. Usually the guy has a straight fringe and is

9

wearing a pastel shirt with a button down collar and short sleeves that flare out like bat wings, so that gives you a bit of a clue, but a list of hobbies and favourite movies would be helpful.

Regardless, I saw Glen on a jetty once and it was odd because it wasn't a jetty in our home town of Adelaide, it was a jetty in a completely different town called Victor Harbour. I'd driven there that morning for a meeting with the Victor Harbour Tourism Council, to discuss website changes, and, after the meeting concluded, I thought, "Well, I'm here now, might as well see some penguins."

I should probably also point out that Victor Harbour is famous for its penguins, it wasn't just a random unrelated impulse. The meeting that morning was partly about penguins, partly about a local motel owner, named Peter, who had been caught drilling peepholes in ceilings. Victor Harbour promotes itself as a family friendly town, and the tourism council was rather concerned about the peephole thing. One of the council members had heard the term *'Once it's on the Internet, it's on there forever,'* and was convinced that anyone typing 'peephole' into Google for the next fifty years would be sent to their *Meet the Locals* page.

The concern had some basis - the *Peephole Peter* story wasn't just a local news thing, it had aired on a major television network show called *Today Tonight* the night before. This was a few years back, and I'm not sure if *Today Tonight* is still a thing, but the show basically consisted of a reporter turning up at people's business or house and asking things like, "Why did you sell fake raffle tickets, Barry? There never was a Ford Focus to be won, was there? Are you going to give everyone their money back? No, don't touch the camera."

The stories varied, they weren't only about fraudulent raffle tickets and peepholes, but the reporter always said the line about touching the camera. It made it more exciting and, if it looked like the person being ambushed wasn't inclined to touch the camera, the cameraman would get really close really quickly and the person would indistinctively raise their hand to stop being hit in the face so the reporter could say it.

Once, the reporter said it to a lady in a wheelchair. I don't recall exactly what the wheelchair lady story was about, but it had something to do with shoplifting. I think she had a secret compartment in her wheelchair.

According to the *Today Tonight* story, a married couple staying at the motel discovered their hole after finding plaster powder on the bed. If it had been me, I probably would have put the hole down to sloppy renovations as nobody wants to see me naked, but I guess the couple contacted *Today Tonight* and said, "I'm pretty sure someone watched us fucking when we stayed in Victor Harbour."

A sting operation was set up and *Today Tonight* lured the motel owner, Peter, into an interview under the guise that his motel had made the *Top Ten Places to Stay in Victor Harbour* list. They created a fake award plaque and a website to add credibility to the ruse. I don't have a transcript, but it went something like:

"Thank you for joining us, Peter. Here's your plaque."
"Thank you. It's an honor."
"Yes, I'm sure it is. Now, how long have you owned the motel?"
"Just over thirty years."
"And how long have you been watching guests though peepholes in the ceiling?"
"What?"
"We've had hidden cameras in the ceiling for two weeks and watched you masturbate a total of twelve times. No, don't touch the camera."

My first thought, when I saw the *Peephole Peter* story, was 'Wait, what was he masturbating to?" Not in a creepy way, more in a 'Did anyone inform the guests?' way. I mean surely someone had to be watching *Today Tonight* and think, "What the fuck, I stayed in that motel last week and nobody warned me about Peter rubbing one out in the ceiling."

I've stayed in a lot of hotel rooms and have done things in them that I'd be mortified to learn anyone witnessed. I've never had sex with a goat or murdered a prostitute, but I did once eat a family-sized pizza on the bed in my underwear.

I've also smoked in every non-smoking room I've ever stayed in. If the room doesn't have a balcony, or at least a window that can be opened, there's a couple of options for smoking cigarettes without leaving too much evidence. The most effective method, which I call *The Vacuum Technique*, is to inhale smoke, hold it, then exhale directly into the toilet bowel at the same time as you flush. The smoke gets pulled down with the water in a vacuum. You have to time it right, and wait for the cistern to fill between puffs, but it beats taking the elevator downstairs. Another highly effective method is *The Soaked Sock Technique*, but it only works properly if you're in the shower and the sock isn't really wearable again. Also, you have to remember to flush the sock down the toilet before housekeeping cleans your room - if it refuses to flush, you can just hide it in the cistern. I've left dozens of cistern socks around the world and I've never been charged a smoking fee. I was once charged for an embarrassing movie purchase, but it wasn't pornography, it was *Spy Kids 3*. Still, there's no need for the lady at the front desk to read out the title when you're checking out and there's people behind you. I should have said something mean about her hair.

The main concern the Victor Harbour Tourism Council had was that the *Meet the Locals* page on their website didn't feature local business owners, it featured penguins, and, much like Glen's chicken dossiers, each penguin had a name and bio with weekly updates on what they'd been up to. Our agency had pitched the idea to the council a year before, and it quickly became the main focus of the website. The updates were surprisingly popular; there was even a day of mourning when Jessica the highly-strung penguin was struck and killed by a boat propellor. The most popular penguin, the penguin who was always getting into some kind of mischief, was named Peter.

"And?"

"You don't see the connection, David?"

"Between Peter the penguin and Peter the ceiling masturbator? No, not really."

"It's the same name."

"Its a very common name."

"It's a very small town."

"Right. So what do you want me do?"

"Delete Peter."

"Delete Peter the penguin?"

"Yes. And all his cookies."

"You don't think that might be an overreaction? Peter is very popular. The update about him stealing a pebble from Susan received over four-thousand views."

"Bradley is also quite popular, we'll just make him the cheeky one."

There's no point arguing with clients who are sixty or older. They're not interested in your opinions because they've already discussed it with Carol in the lunchroom and Carol agreed with them. Boards and councils make the worst clients because everyone is old and senile and the simplest issues become complicated disasters so they can look like problem solvers. It's all they have. That and their 1974 hairstyles.

"And next on the agenda is the ant situation in the kitchen. Any suggestions?"

"If we pour fifty bottles of maple syrup on the floor, the ants might gorge themselves to death."

"Excellent. Take the lead on that project and have a report ready for the next board meeting. Something with graphs and maybe clipart of ants."

"I could make the graphs out of ants."

"Clipart ants or real ants?"

"I'll try both."

Nobody gave a fuck about Bradley; his neck feathers were scruffy and he had weird eyes, while Peter's sudden disappearance caused far more public outcry than expected. There were angry phone calls to the council and a local store started selling *Where's Peter?* t-shirts, so Peter was brought back as Petra - Victor Harbour's first transgender penguin.

It wasn't well received. There are a lot of old people in Victor Harbour and I guess they got together, probably in a park or something, and put together a petition to have Petra's name changed back to Peter. This resulted in the LGBT community holding a march with signs that said, "We love you the way you are, Petra!" and, "Penguin Pride!" which gained National news coverage.

The tourism council was pleased; the news coverage had distracted everyone from the *Peephole Peter* story, and site updates about Petra's brave journey were receiving thousands more hits per day than any other page. A Photoshopped image of Petra holding a Birkin bag received half a million views. Then someone shot and killed Petra with an air rifle and the *Meet the Locals* page was replaced with photos of whales.

Also, just in case you were wondering what happened to the motel owner, he sold the motel and moved to Malaysia. Apparently peeping is a misdemeanor and only carries a fine. It could also be argued that the shame inflicted by *Today Tonight* was punishment enough - he'd lived in Victor Harbour for forty years. Interestingly, two years later, Peter was punched in a bar in Tanjung Piandang, for singing loudly, and died from a hemorrhagic stroke. I'm not sure how any of that connects but it took four hours of research so there's no way I wasn't going to include it.

This was all well after I saw Glen on the jetty of course. The tourism council tangent took up far more pages than I thought it would, but if I'd just written, "I was in a different town and decided to look for penguins," you would have thought, "What?"

The jetty was only a short stroll from the tourism council building and mostly empty - I wouldn't have gone if it was busy as I prefer humans in groups of six or less. It's the noise mainly. There were no penguins, just a couple of people fishing and, further along, an old lady in a one-piece swimsuit and a skinny guy in board shorts were jumping off the guardrail into the water. There was a ladder near their jumping point and I watched them climb out and jump twice again in the time it took me to get closer. As I approached, the old lady climbed the guardrail, yelled, "I'm not the rotten egg!" and leaped laughing. The skinny guy climbed the guardrail and was about to jump, when I said, "Glen?"

"Oh, hi, David."
"Hi. What's going on?"
"Not much. What about you?"
"No, I mean what's going on? Who is that? Is that your mum?"
"No, that's just a lady I gave free eggs to."
"What?"

The old lady yelled, "Come on, Glen, let's swim back to shore!" and, before I could interrogate Glen further, he gave me a cheery wave goodbye, jumped in, and swam off with the old lady.

I'm going to note here that my partner Holly read the last few paragraphs and stated, "What's so odd about jumping off a jetty? I think it's nice, it sounds like they were having fun!" so she must have missed the bits about it being an entirely different town and Glen jumping off a jetty with an old lady he gave free eggs to. There can't be any other explanation. Or maybe this kind of thing is normal in Holly's world and everyone's bumping into people they know on jetties in different towns with their egg friend.

I intended to ask Glen about the jetty thing the next time I saw him, but it was several months before I bumped into him again - in a supermarket buying way too many lemons for one person to possibly use - and I forgot to ask him about the jetty because of all the lemons and the fact that he had a prosthetic hand. It was rubber but it had some kind of mechanism inside that allowed him to pick up things. Like lemons. Apparently he'd cut his hand while shovelling chicken poo out of a window, it became infected, and he ended up hospitalised. I think he had the same thing tourists get when they get splashed while attending a Hindu ritual on the banks of the Ganges. To add to his woes, while Glen was in hospital having appendages lopped off, his landlord discovered the chickens and evicted him.

It wasn't one of those "we warned you you were on thin ice" evictions where you get fourteen day's notice. The landlord just gave the chickens to a Greek neighbour and threw Glen's belongings into a dumpster. He also gave Glen a $4,800 invoice to replace the floorboards, so Glen changed his telephone number and moved into his grandparent's shed.

I felt bad for Glen, which is why I lent him money and built him a website, but really, he should have pushed a couple of mowers before starting a lawn mowing service to see if his robot hand was up to the task.

Also, I looked up Glen on Facebook while I was writing this - partly to see how he was doing but mainly for closure about the jetty thing - but his last post was in 2014. It was regarding Malaysian Airlines flight 370 and time rips - apparently the plane landed in 1957 and that's how microchip technology was discovered. I sent Glen a message, but he didn't reply, so I messaged a couple of people on his 'friends' list, asking about his wellbeing. His sister messaged me back to let me know Glen now lives on a farm with lots of chickens. No, not really, he died in a go-karting accident.

Distractions

There's a bird in the office!

It's the most exciting thing to have happened at the agency in months and everyone has dropped all pretence of working to join the adventure. There have been dozens of suggestions and some synchronised poster tube waving, but the bird (either a small sparrow or a fat finch, there's some debate) doesn't appear to want to leave.

Update

The bird has a name now. It's Gary. Gary our account manager isn't pleased with the bird having the same name and seems to have missed the whole point of naming it Gary by reacting exactly as expected. He's at the "We'll just see what Kate has to say about this!" stage already.

Also the term, "Which Gary?" is now an established response to any mention of either Gary.

"Gary's in Kate's office."

"Which Gary?"

"Old Gary."

Update

Gary has a house. Bird Gary, not Old Gary. Old Gary also has a house, but it's not as nice as Bird Gary's. Old Gary's house is a two bedroom, one bathroom, brick bungalow in a shitty neighborhood. Bird Gary's house, constructed from the finest foam board, is a modern take on Wright's *Fallingwater* and has a prime rafter position overlooking the studio. His lower balcony doubles as a feeding station, with recessed spray-adhesive-cap water and food bowls, while the interior is lined with shredded canary-yellow photocopier paper.

It was easier to persuade Bird Gary to seek refuge in his house than it was to get him to go outside, but it still took a bit of teamwork.

Companies spend a lot of money on those staff team-building retreats where you have to make a plank bridge or something equally as stupid. They should just release a bird in the office.

At the last team-building retreat we attended, Jodie, our senior designer, and Melissa, our 'first impressions director', argued during a raft-building exercise and Melissa took an oar to the face. I don't recall exactly what Melissa said to enrage Jodie, but it was something to do with buoyancy and weight distribution. Jodie's been eating for two lately; sad Jodie and hungry Jodie. She was doing Ozempic injections for a while, but it turned out to be a cheap Chinese knockoff that was actually some kind of bean juice. She ordered it online and had to use Venmo, so you'd think that would have been a red flag. There's always something sketchy going on if you have to pay with Venmo. It's mainly just for poppers, sandwich bag weed, and Denny's parking lot handjobs.

"What kind of beans?"
"I don't know, just beans."
"I didn't even know beans had juice."
"Everything has juice if you squeeze hard enough."

Kate, our HR director, made Jodie apologise to Melissa, but instead of accepting the apology, Melissa spat a huge gob of spit and blood in Jodie's face. Some went in Jodie's mouth because she always has it open. That's not another jab at Jodie's eating habits, she always has her mouth slightly open like she's doing a little yawn or is about to say the word 'up'. Mike, our creative director, doesn't like her being in client meetings because "nobody wants to stare across the table at fish girl."

There have been no arguments regarding Bird Gary; Jodie and Melissa prepared a multi-grain bread and oatmeal treat for him in the kitchen together, and Jodie held the ladder while Melissa climbed up to place it in his food bowl. There was even a high five after she climbed back down as if to say, "Go Team Bird!"

Update

According to Kate, there's no rule against naming the bird Gary, but we can't refer to human Gary as Old Gary, as it's age discrimination and harassment.

Old Gary is now Gary 2, and Bird Gary is Gary 1.

Gary 2 is arguing that he should be Gary 1, as he's been here longer, but at this point it would just confuse Gary 1 to have to go through another name change.

Update

It's nice having Gary 1 in the office. It's added a sense of tranquility to the environment; like we're in a tropical rainforest near a waterfall. The natural sounds balance out the *mermmmmmm* of the water cooler and *chukala chuckala clunk* of the photocopier getting jammed. It's probably as close to Zen as we're going to get here. Occasionally, the tranquility is interrupted by Gary 1 getting a bit close during his investigative studio flights (Ben is a screamer), but for the most part he stays close to his house, chirping and jumping between rafters.

Not a lot of work is getting done, but it never is - distractions account for around 70% of each working day and they're rarely as exciting as a bird in the office. Yesterday, I had to entertain myself for an hour with a pen spring.

The last exciting distraction was two months ago, when we had a fire in the kitchen, and that could have been a lot better. I was hoping the whole building would burn down and we'd get a decent break while it was being rebuilt, but Kate ruined that for everyone by working out how to use the fire extinguisher. We're meant to have a 'fire marshal' check the extinguishers and smoke alarms every year for insurance purposes, but going by the rip tags on the extinguishers, the last time that happened was on July 18, 2003. Occasionally when a smoke alarm starts chirping, someone manages to find a 9 volt battery, but usually we just disconnect the wires.

The smoke alarm in the kitchen has been completely missing since it chirped last year. Walter knocked it down with a broom handle and hid it under some leaves. The rule around here is 'if you break it, hide it or say nothing and hope someone else thinks they broke it'. The rule doesn't apply to Mike of course, when he fucks something up, it's always due to someone else's incompetence:

From: Mike Campbell
Date: Tuesday 12 March 2024 12.37pm
To: All Staff
Subject: Kitchen fire

It's easy to blame the kitchen fire on the person who happened to be using the toaster oven at the time, but the fact remains, there wouldn't have been a fire if we had a decent toaster oven.

Who buys a Hamilton Beach toaster oven? Are we poor?

In future, all kitchen appliances purchased for this agency are to approved by me. If I see another Hamilton Beach product in the kitchen, it will be immediately thrown in the dumpster.

It's not just a brand thing, it's a safety thing. And yes, before you bother asking, this email *is* directed at you Melissa. Someone could have been badly burnt.

Mike

....

It was technically the second time Mike has caused an office fire. He gave his partner Patrick a candle making kit for Christmas last year, and Patrick got a little carried away with the whole thing. As a professional artisan candlemaker, Patrick planned to start small with stalls at county fairs, then sell the brand for billions once Gwyneth Paltrow started selling it on Goop.

It's good to have a hobby other than masturbation, but you should probably check if you're any good at it before spending five grand on pots, wax, and oils. The candles sputtered a lot. Patrick blamed the wicks, but I suspect the 50/50 ratio of wax and scented oils may have had something do with it. I'm not a candle scientist, but I'm fairly sure they're meant to have a thicker consistency than toothpaste. They definitely smelled though. Even unlit they filled a room with scent. When lit, the scent was a bit much and it looked like someone was welding, but by the time you realised you had made a huge mistake and doused the flame, it was too late. If you were lucky, you'd just have a couple of hundred wax sputters over a four-foot radius. If you were unlucky, they'd be on fire. Regardless, your room was going to smell like Oud & Rhubarb for the next month.

Oud & Rhubarb was Patrick's signature scent, but he had three others. To create a point of difference from his competitors, he'd decided his scents needed to be unique and unusual - regardless of whether the combinations balanced well or caused seizures.

"I quite like the Oud & Rhubarb; it's like having pie at your grandma's house after a day of fighting forest fires. I'm not sure about Peppermint & Guacamole though, it's a bit 'Christmas in Cancún', and Onion & Licorice blinded me for several minutes."

"Right, well, when I said I welcome feedback, I meant *positive* feedback, so I'll just ignore everything you said. You must have some kind of disease that makes you smell things wrong. Also, you're stupid and have no fashion sense."

It was Mushroom & Tobacco that set Mike's desk ablaze. It contained actual tobacco which acted like hundreds of little wicks. The flame was about two-feet high and sounded like a hot air balloon burner. Also, candles aren't meant to boil over. It's just not a thing. There wasn't a huge amount of damage, but the side of Mike's monitor melted and a section of ceiling above his desk turned black. It could have been worse, apparently one of Patrick's candles exploded.

Luckily, nobody bought any. Patrick only went to one local market; he made Mike sit at a booth with him for two hours until they had an argument over why the candles weren't selling, and Patrick kicked over their table. The problem wasn't that the candles were dangerous - people wouldn't know that until it was lit - it was the price. Scented oils are ridiculously expensive and the candles had around eight bottles in each. Nobody wants to pay $60 for a candle. You can get them for $4.99 at TJ Maxx. Patrick gave up on candle making after that and is into soap making now. I tried his Birch Tar & Tumeric body scrub and it left me with third-degree burns.

Mike is actually away at the moment. He's with Patrick in Hartford, Connecticut, at the 26th Annual

Handcrafted Soap and Cosmetic Conference. It's a four-day event with guest speakers and exhibitions. Mike attempted to get out of going, but Patrick threatened to leave him as he can't be with someone who isn't supportive of his passions. Apparently Mike attended a three-hour seminar on lye temperature this morning, and is currently in a TED talk about salves.

From: Mike Campbell
Date: Wednesday 15 May 2024 1.27pm
To: David Thorne, Kate Routledge
Subject: Emergency

David and Kate,

David, at 2.10pm today, send me a message that Moen is threatening to go to a competing agency and I have to meet with them tomorrow.

Kate, call me a few minutes later and say the same thing. I'll say that I can't meet them tomorrow because I'm here supporting my partner, and then you'll say Moen are only in town for one day and they've been talking to Starfish. I'll say something about how that would financially cripple us and you'll sigh and say, "I know, we need you, Mike."

You'll be on speaker so don't say anything stupid. Just make it convincing. I can't do any more soap things.

Mike

....

It's lucky Mike isn't here as there's no way he'd let us keep Gary 1. Mike wears outrageously expensive suits that can only be tongue-cleaned by specially bred cats, and Gary 1 poos a lot. We expected some poo, but we weren't expecting Gary 1 to poo while flying; it spreads it, like splashed paint, and he's gone through a lot of his multi-grain bread and oatmeal.

"He's so tiny. Where does he put it all?"
"On the walls mostly, there's also a big splatter on the photocopier and a weird green and grey one on Gary 2's keyboard. He's going to be pissed when he gets back from his doctor's appointment."

Gary 2 has a doctor's appointment at least once a month. He's at that age where the grandkids only visit to steal pills from his bathroom cabinet. Even Gary's desk has about twenty pill containers on it. I check the labels occasionally to see if there's anything worth taking, but they're usually just antibiotics and anti-inflammatories. He does have Alprazolam in his drawer, but it just puts me to sleep. Apparently it's prescribed to manage anxiety, so I can't imagine what Gary 2 would be like if he wasn't on them. He yells at everyone and everything: plants, faucet pressure, microwave beeps - and refuses to sit with his back to the door in meetings because "That's how they got my cousin Steve."

David 2.10 PM

Mike, Moen is threatening to go to a competing agency. You have to meet with them tomorrow.

Mike 2.11PM

Are you serious? I can't leave now. It would be unfair to Patrick.

David 2.12 PM

Okay. I'm sure a couple of days won't make any difference. Just enjoy your time in Hartford. Have you visited the Mark Twain House & Museum yet?

Mike 2.13PM

...

Update

Mike is flying back this evening. Not because of a fake client emergency - Kate refused to participate in his ruse - but because he tumbled down a flight of stairs and hurt his leg. I'm guessing he threw himself down the stairs to avoid tomorrow's exhibition of Victorian Era soap molds. It wouldn't be the first time Mike has chosen injury over attendance; he once made me punch him in the face so he wouldn't have to go to Patrick's community theatre group production of *Guys & Dolls*. He said he'd been mugged. My first punch was just hard enough not to be *quite* hard enough, so I'd get a second punch.

Update

The sense of tranquility has been broken. Jodie asked, "What if Gary 1 is a girl and she has babies waiting for her?" so now there's a dark element to keeping him/her here. The office is basically divided into two factions: those demanding Gary 1's release, and those who haven't had their desk pooed on yet. Gary 2 returned to the office and suggested killing Gary 1, but nobody cares what Gary 2 has to say. I stopped listening to him in 2019 when he asked if I could use a 'jazzier' typeface than Helvetica.

Update

A vote was taken, by show of hands, and Gary 1 is being evicted. His house has been removed and the door leading to the courtyard is being held open by five reams of canary-yellow photocopier paper.

All it's done so far is let flies in, and they're dumpster flies, which are the worst kind of flies. Our office mostly just throws paper in the dumpster, but we share it with two other businesses in the building and one makes 'edible arrangements'.

For those not familiar with edible arrangements, they're similar to a flower arrangement, but made out of fruit slices that strangers have touched and breathed on. I was certain the business would be bankrupt within a few months, as nobody on the planet has ever said, "Ooh, slimy fruit on sticks. That's much better than flowers!", but apparently there's a demographic of people who think, "I should probably send Helen something for her birthday but I really don't like her enough to send flowers. If only there was something similar but with E.coli..."

Sometimes when they have an order cancelled, a lady named June brings the edible arrangement over for us to eat - which is very annoying. We can't throw it in the dumpster, as they might see it, so we have to deconstruct the disgusting thing and flush the chunks down a toilet. Walter, our junior designer, once chanced a couple of slices of pineapple, then spent the rest of the afternoon in the bathroom making ghost sounds. Ashley, our newest designer, took him bottles of water so he wouldn't become dehydrated.

Oh, I should probably mention Ashley and Walter were an item, then they broke up, then got back together, then broke up, then moved in together, then broke up, and are now engaged. Walter proposed while they were shopping for an iRobot at Best Buy.

"That's not exactly romantic, Walter."
"I was going to do it earlier, while we were feeding the chickens, but my nephew kept throwing sticks at us."
"What?"
"He's really annoying. He goes to one of those special schools for kids who punch holes in walls."
"Okay, but... chickens?"
"My auntie's chickens. She has a farm."
"And how is feeding chickens romantic?"
"It isn't. Especially when someone's throwing sticks at you."

Update

A Hansel & Gretel style multi-grain bread and oatmeal temptation trail leading to the courtyard isn't working, so the poster tube waving system has been reimplemented.

Walter also found a YouTube video of hawks squawking, so is standing on top of a ladder holding his phone up while it plays. Ashley is instructing Walter to be careful as that's always helpful.

There's no statistics on how many ladder accidents are avoided each year by being told to be careful, but it's probably in the millions.

Update

Gary 1 has left the building. It was a combination of poster tube waving, clapping, yelling, hawk squawks, and a very surprised DHL courier opening the front door that finally convinced Gary 1 there might be better options outside. The courier looked more panicked than surprised really; it's probably not something you mentally prep for when you enter a business, and I doubt they cover it in courier school.

"And that's what you do when a dog chases you. Any questions? Yes Roger?"

"What if you enter a business and everyone's clapping and yelling and waving poster tubes and there's a guy on top of a ladder playing a YouTube video of a hawk squawking?"

"We've spoken about this, Roger. There are people here who want to learn and everyone's getting a little tired of your nonsense."

Update

There's something different about the office now. It's the same office it was before Gary 1 visited, but somehow it's *more* officey. The hums and clunks are louder and I can even hear the clock.

It's an old clock, about eighteen inches in diameter, and I assume it's been here since the sixties when this building was a boot factory. It doesn't have a battery, it has wires that go straight into the wall, so there's probably been a few times when someone has gone to swap it for a newer clock and then changed their mind because they didn't want to deal with the wires. I don't think I've ever noticed it makes a sound before. Each tick is sharp and clear, there's no tocks.

It's likely somebody once sat where I'm sitting, doing boot stuff, listening to the same clock. They're probably dead now.

Update

We took a vote and are getting an office turtle. We're going to name it Gary 2 and change Gary 2's name to Gary 3.

And Then the Robots
Attacked

My partner Holly and I have an established system for who gets to choose what we watch on television. It's a turn-based system, but it's always Holly's turn. If I indicate any objection to her choice, Holly states, "Just give it five minutes."

It's step one of a four-step process comprising of:

1. "Just give it five minutes."

2. "Just give it another five minutes."

3. "Shhh, I'm invested now."

4. "That was just episode one. It's a four-part series."

For the most part, I don't mind not having the responsibility of choice. I don't like scrolling through fifteen different streaming services - all with different interfaces - attempting to find something vaguely watchable. Most of the streaming services don't even use the proper cover image, they make their own, so you'll be scrolling and think, "Ooh, what's this?"

but then it turns out to be *Friends* or a documentary about Alexandre-Ferdinand Godefroy, the inventor of the hair dryer. Choice *without* responsibility is difficult enough without having to consider another person's likes and dislikes. Not that Holly has that problem.

"Oh, you're not in the mood for a historical drama about a Scottish woman's fight for reparations from a greedy peat-moss company after her husband drowned in a bog? You should have said something earlier. There's another show I wanted to watch about cotton."

Really I'm just thankful to be watching television, whatever's on, as it means I'm not doing something else. The worst part about any relationship is having to do things other than watch television. Sometimes Holly makes me go to the supermarket or out to dinner and I think to myself, "Is a relationship really worth this?" You have to shower and put on pants and look at the sun. Once when we were at the supermarket and there wasn't any room in the cart, Holly made me carry a watermelon. People look at you when you carry a watermelon; they assume you went shopping and got everything you needed and then decided to get a watermelon.

I don't like people looking at me even when I'm not carrying a watermelon. People should be more task orientated and less inquisitive. Some of them even have a good gander at the items in your cart as you pass. How the fuck is it anyone's business what I have in my cart? Eyes up, bitch, stop looking at my frozen waffles and hotdog buns. Shopping carts should be translucent and there should be partitions at the checkout so that people can't stare at your groceries as they make their journey along the conveyor belt. It's like they're analysing your meal plan for the week and judging you for all the bread. I usually make a little fort using packs of toilet paper and paper towels to block the view of smaller items, but you have to put the bread on last or it will end up at the bottom of a bag of cans.

Also, while somehow still on the subject, you should always avoid shopping at a Food Lion supermarket. It's definitely the worst supermarket chain I have experienced while living in the United States. It's dirty, most of the employees are registered sex offenders, and the majority of products are three weeks past their expiry date. I've been to three different Food Lions and they're all the same. Martin's is a better supermarket but their shelves give you electric shocks.

Having waived the responsibility of choice in regards to what to watch, I have no right to complain or criticize. I still do though, often it's impossible not to. Holly once chose a movie about a lady who fell in love with a fish. I challenge anyone to sit quietly through that. My criticisms need to be short and quick, otherwise they will be interrupted with a 'Shhhhh!" so I have a default sentence that covers most situations and expresses exactly how I feel:

"And then the robots attacked."

It's just five words, so if I say it fast there's no time for Holly to shhhh me, and it says everything I need it to. At it's basic level, it says, "This movie is dreadful and the only thing that would save it is if robots attack in the next scene," but it also says, "I hate everyone in this movie and I wish robots would kill them," and, "I'd rather be watching a movie with robots in it."

There's hundreds of movies that would be greatly improved if robots attacked. Here's ten off the top of my head... **Note:** I don't pay much attention to the movies Holly chooses - I spend most of the time on my phone - so the character's names may be wrong and the dialogue improvised, but the point stands.

Driving Miss Daisy

"Slow down, Geoff, it's a bit bumpy."
"Sorry, Miss Daisy."
And then the robots attacked.

The Notebook

"Thanks for building me a house and taking me for a boat ride. There sure were a lot of swans."
"I love you."
"Okay."
And then the robots attacked.

Little Women

"Do you have time to talk about my feelings for forty-five minutes?"
"Of course, I'll pop the kettle on."
And then the robots attacked.

The Color Purple

"That sure is a lovely shade of purple."
"Thank you, Oprah."
And then the robots attacked.

Girls

And then the robots attacked.

Emily in Paris

"What's that, Emily?"
"It's an emoji, the latest thing in social media."
"You're so cool. Will you have sex with me?"
"Hashtag yes."
And then the robots attacked.

La La Land

"I sure do love jazz."
And then the robots attacked.

The Lake House

"Dear Keanu, how's things in 2004?"
"Pretty good. Doing a bit of painting. Hey, can you send me a list of winning lottery numbers?"
And then the robots attacked.

Eat Pray Love

"Hmm, is this really about spaghetti or are you just planning to sleep around?"
"Bit of both."
And then the robots attacked.

Bridget Jones's Diary

"Dear Diary, I'm feeling sad about my weight."
And then the robots attacked.

It should be noted that application of "And then the robot's attacked" isn't limited to movies and television shows. It can be used in office meetings, during relationship discussions, at bluegrass music festivals, and whenever anyone tells you about a dream they had three nights ago about someone you've never met doing something you don't care about.

There are also instances where application may seem appropriate, but aren't, like maybe a funeral, and it can only be used in conjunction with waiving the responsibility of choice. You can't use it if you chose the movie/show/activity - admitting you made a bad choice means you have to hand over the remote control. There's no restraint for the remote control holder at that point, they can watch what they want because your last choice was shit. You're watching a nine-part series about quilting.

"And this panel was added by my great grandmother Ethel. It's a flour sack coloured with beets."
"And then the robots attacked."
"No, you don't get to say that after *Rebel Moon*."

Benefits of waiving responsibility of choice almost aways outweigh the recriminations of choosing. This applies to restaurants, furniture, travel…

The one time I took responsibility for choosing a travel destination, we ended up in a cult. It wasn't like the Kool-Aid type of cult where everyone has to wear the same sneakers, but we did have to eat at a big table with everyone else.

It was Holly's fault. Making me choose a vacation destination when she knows I don't like browser tabs is just irresponsible. I pick the first place on the first page so I can do something else.

"Did you research the place?"
"Of course I did."
"There's a government warning advising tourists not to travel to that part of Mexico."
"We'll be fine. They have a compound."

Sleep

I'm a big fan of sleep. I read somewhere that you need less as you get older, but I think it's more of a tick-shaped curve. You're forced to sleep as a child, evade it in your teens, then crave it as an adult. At some point you have nothing better to do; the staff at the senior living facility have heard all your stories, nobody wants to play Cribbage, and someone stole your teeth.

"Exciting news, Mister Thorne."
"I have a visitor?"
"No, we're having mashed carrot for dinner."
"Okay, definitely wake me up for that."

I'd sleep half the day if I could, just split it into two parts - the bed part and the not bed part. Years back, I lived in a studio apartment - with just an everything room and a bathroom, no other rooms - and I could reach the coffeemaker on the kitchen bench from my bed. Now I have different rooms for different things and most of the things aren't beds.

It should be a natural progression of age that you slowly replace all of your furniture with beds. I don't even know why we have a dining table and chairs; we only use them once a year for Christmas dinner, and nobody enjoys it. I like watching television while I'm eating, not watching other people eating. I've seen festive scenes on television where attractive families wearing colourful sweaters laugh gaily as they pass bowls of mashed potato, but there's not a lot of that happening at our Christmas dinners. It's mostly just statements about how long it's been since we last used the dining table. If good meals are based on good company and good conversation, the best we can hope for is a quick meal.

We essentially have an entire room devoted to one hour of one day each year. The dining table was also used for a jigsaw puzzle once, but nobody here ever wants to go through that again. It had a lot of trees. I think it was a Bavarian castle. The living room gets used a lot more than the dining room, but it's basically just for watching television, so it would definitely make sense to swap the couch for a big bed in there. Maybe two for when we have visitors so it isn't awkward. There's not a lot of room in the kitchen, but a single bed would fit. That way I could have quick kip while I'm waiting for pasta to cook.

The main reason I'm a big fan of sleep is that I don't get any. I haven't had a decent night's sleep in years. It's not insomnia, I have no problem falling asleep, it's because we share a bed with a Boston terrier.

If you haven't lived with a Boston terrier, you may be thinking, "So just don't let it sleep on the bed." Hahaha, sigh. That's not how any of this works. It's our fault, we welcomed him onto the bed when he was a puppy - he needed to be close to people at all times - but we thought he'd grow out of it, that it was just a puppy thing. It isn't, it's a Boston terrier thing. Also, when I say 'close to people', I don't mean 'in the general vicinity', I mean '*on* people'. Depending on how horizontal you happen to be, this can mean your lap, chest, or face. I'm generally fully horizontal in bed.

You may also be thinking, "Boston terrier's aren't that big, how much room could one possibly take up in bed?" It's all the room, but that's not the only issue, Boston terriers fart constantly. I'm sure there are plenty of breeds of dog that fart a lot, but note that I used the word 'constantly', not 'often'. Again, its a small breed, so how bad can the farts be? It's quite astonishing actually, these aren't the kind of farts you can just pull your t-shirt up over your nose and wait out, they're tear-inducing dense clouds that permeate even the thickest of fabrics.

Additionally, due to their short snouts and small nostrils, Boston terriers snore like a 400 pound 50-year-old man with a deviated septum. They're also not great at regulating temperature so will change sleeping positions around 400 times throughout the night.

Here are a few of our Boston terrier's most common sleeping positions. ***Note:*** Neither Holly nor I look like this, I have better hair and rarely wear pants to bed, but the positions are correct. Holly commandeers around 70% of the bed to accommodate her bicycle riding position:

Position 1: *The VR Helmet*   **Position 2:** *The Rice Cooker*

Position 3: *The Everybody Was Kung-Fu Fighting*

Position 4: *The Don't Forget Your Scarf*

Position 5: *The This Is Why We Shouldn't Feed Him Table Food*

Position 6: *The I'm Up Here and You're Down There*

51

Turtle

We have an office turtle! The plan was to name him Gary 2 and change our account manager's name from Gary 2 to Gary 3, but Gary 2 said he would poison the turtle if we named it Gary 2, so we named the turtle Gary Gary and Gary 2 became Gary Gary Gary. It was funny for about two hours and then became really annoying so we changed Gary Gary's name to Flipper. It wasn't my suggestion but I'm fine with the decision. Mainly because when you hear and say Gary too many times it loses all meaning and you forget how to say it and question if it's even a word. Like yolk.

"Gary Gary or Gary Gary Gary?"
"Gary Gry Grygrrry."

Also, one of Flipper's flippers is deformed - it's half the size of his other three - which is how Melissa came up with his name. It's kind of like calling someone with a deformed arm Arm, but Flipper isn't likely to file a discrimination complaint...

Turtles

We have *three* office turtles! Despite having Flipper on the front desk for less than a day, Melissa has developed a tight telepathic bond with him and he communicated that he was lonely and needs a friend otherwise he will be sad and stop eating and probably die.

I drove Melissa to the pet store as she can only drive her car in peak-hour traffic. She lost her license a few weeks back, for six months, and will only drive when there's lots of other cars around her. It's like cattle staying together; a safety in numbers thing. Or maybe more like a raffle, the more tickets there are in a hat, the less likely you are to be picked. Actually, they're both the same thing.

Regardless, for Melissa, it's not about legality, it's about mitigated risk vs. catching a bus. The first time she caught a bus to work, a baby threw up on the back of her head. She washed it out in the kitchen sink with Dawn dish soap, but her hair went frizzy, so she tried moisturising it with hand lotion, then caught an Uber home with a tea towel wrapped around her head like an old Russian babushka. She Ubered for a few weeks but then Mike found out she was charging the rides to the company credit card and yelled at her until she cried and banged her head on her desk.

I mean, I get it, there's no way I'd catch a bus to work, but maybe don't throw back thirty jello shots then drive your Subaru Crosstrek onto a tennis court.

People were playing at the time and one of them took away her keys so she couldn't escape. The excuse she gave the judge was that she thought the jello shots would take half an hour to melt in her stomach, and her house was only a twenty minute drive away, which means she wasn't purposely driving under the influence. If anything, she's the victim here, of misinformation, and who's going to pay for all the scratches on her Crosstrek?

I didn't mind going to the pet store; we're not real busy at work. I spent most of today playing with a retractable tape measure and watching YouTube videos of Indonesian men digging swimming pools in a jungle. There must be money in the jungle pool business because I've seen at least thirty different videos. The main problem I have with the videos is that there's no filtration system for the water. It has to get a bit of gammy after a week or two. Also, what happens if a snake falls in?

"Which turtle?"
"You can choose, Melissa. I only came in to play with the ferrets."
"We should get two and pick one each."
"Okay. I'm going to name mine Good Looking Ben."

Flipper, Good Looking Ben, and Flappy seem happy with their new home. We bought a larger aquarium at the pet store and around $600 worth of pebbles, plastic plants, and an island for them to climb onto. The island has a little palm tree on it and a couple of beach chairs. It's not the theme I would have gone for but it will annoy Mike. Also, the aquarium seems a lot bigger on the front desk than it looked in the store and Melissa's head is magnified through it. She always has a 'Oh no, what the fuck do you want?' look on her face, and now it's in big screen format.

Ben doesn't appreciate the fact that unlike Gary 2, he doesn't have to change his name. It's just Good Looking Ben and Ben. He's welcome to get his own turtle and name it whatever he likes. Also, everybody hates the name Flappy apart from Melissa.

Update

We have *four* office turtles. Ben drove to the pet store and bought one for the sole purpose of naming it David Thorne Is Ugly - which is just an unimaginative version of my turtle's name and kind of weak. I'm going out to buy another turtle so I can name it Creative Ben.

Who Knew Go-Karting Was So Dangerous?

I knew a guy in Australia, named Glen, who died in a go-karting accident. Yes, it's the same Glen from the earlier story; it would be a bizarre coincidence to know two Glen's who died in go-karting accidents.

I have known *three* Trevors who died in automobile accidents, but the name Trevor is pretty common in Australia and so are automobile accidents. Most Australian's fall into one of two driver categories: drunk or angry. It's also difficult to keep your eyes on the road when you're punching your missus or reaching back to grope a passed-out passenger in the back seat. Groping accounts for 23% of taxi accidents in Australia.

"We're here. That will be $34.50 thanks."
"What about the grope discount?"
"Sorry?"
"I was awake through most of it."
"Fine."

I might receive a few emails from Australians for the previous text - something along the lines of, "You're not being much of an ambassador, maybe ease up on the groping jokes and talk more about prawns and koalas," or, "I'm an Adelaide taxi driver and I haven't groped anyone in ages", but I don't care. Nobody is paying me to be a good ambassador and everyone I know in America is tired of me extolling Australia's virtues.

"Our health care system is way better than yours."
"Can you buy a shotgun at Walmart?"
"No."
"Well, shut the fuck up then."

I wasn't aware Glen was into go-karting so I have no idea if it was his first time or he was a regular. I've always assumed go-karting is more of an activity for young children and stoned teenagers than adults. I don't like bumper-cars unless I'm the only one doing the bumping, and I've only ever driven the outdoor-track type of go-karts twice in my life.

The first time was at a school friend's birthday party in 1983, and the next time was in 2015 during the second, and last, vacation I took with Holly and her parents to Emerald Isle, North Carolina.

For as long as Holly can remember, her parents - Tom and Maria - have booked a beach house on Emerald Isle for a week during summer. It was the only family vacation they took each year and there was always a lot of excitement in the weeks leading up to the trip. Coolers were cleaned, beach umbrellas were tested, ventilated caps were purchased.

I joined them the first summer after I moved to America and it didn't go well. I wrote about that vacation in an earlier book, so I won't go into detail here, but basically Tom and Maria took their cats to the beach and one of them, Bob, died during the six-hour car ride. They buried him on the beach but some kids dug up Bob the next morning and chased each other with him. Attempting to protect Tom and Maria from witnessing this, I ran after the kids, retrieved Bob, secured a hefty rock under his collar, and yeeted him out into the surf. No disrespect to Bob was intended, and if Tom hadn't later waded out into the water and yanked on what he thought was rope, he would never have known. Who yanks ropes in the water? After beating a crab off Bob's face with a flip-flop, Tom accused me of ruining the family vacation and stabbed an inflatable killer whale that had taken me almost two hours to blow up with my mouth.

Nobody went to Emerald Isle the next year. Tom and Maria spent the money on a gazebo instead. It was a shitty little gazebo, I think they got it from Home Depot. It could almost fit two people but only if you pointed your knees away from each other. Someone eventually stole it, so that should give you some idea of how small it was.

I felt bad that it was the first year in decades Holly's family hadn't gone to Emerald Isle, so I booked a beach house for the following summer. It took Tom some convincing to go, but I promised to be on my best behaviour and bought him a fold-up beach chair with four drink holders in the armrests and a padded headrest as enticement. I forgot to take it, but it's the thought that counts.

It's a long drive to Emerald Isle, so we left early, but Holly needs to stop at every rest-stop because her bladder is the size of a Lego man's head. She also always asks, "Are you hungry?" two minutes into any trip. It doesn't matter where we're going, it could be a quick drive to Lowe's to buy potting mix. Then, when I reply, "No, not really," she says, "Okay," in a way that indicates she's a bit disappointed and was hoping I'd say, "Yes, let's get Qdoba!" for the first time in fourteen years of being asked.

"You're not even slightly hungry?"

"Not at all."

"I could probably eat. Only if you want to though."

"I'm good."

"I'll just eat something later then. I'll be okay. I might wait in the car while you get the potting mix though, I'm feeling a bit light-headed... whoa, I think I just blacked out for a moment. Do you hear bells?"

It was late afternoon by the time we arrived, so it was decided beach activities could wait until the following day and we'd head out to play mini-golf. It wasn't my decision, I'm not a mini-golfer, but I'd agreed to be a more amicable version of myself for the vacation. A version that played mini-golf and Trivial Pursuit and didn't complain about the smell of unchanged kitty litter boxes. David 2.0 - the beach edition.

Mini-golf at Emerald Isle has always been a 'family tradition' thing for Holly and her parents. It's one of the things you have to do, along with buying flip-flops at Bert's and eating Mexican every night. The Mexican thing wasn't totally by choice, there are only five restaurants on Emerald Isle and they're all Mexican. There is an Olive Garden over a bridge, but it's a 45-minute wait and they don't have fresh basil.

Holly's older brother, Marty, used to join them on vacation, but he moved to Philadelphia to become a cheese taster. I've met him a couple times and he's really not memorable enough to write a description for. Just imagine the fat kid in *Charlie and the Chocolate Factory* but with darker hair - the original movie, not the Jack Sparrow version. I haven't seen the Jack Sparrow version, or the newer one with the chin guy, mostly because I don't give a fuck about chocolate factories.

Marty is a mini-golf champion. I know this because there are fourteen mini-golf trophies on Tom and Maria's bookshelf with his name on them. They sell them at the mini-golf shop.

There are no trophies on the bookshelf with Holly's name on them, and it quickly became obvious why. Mini-golf requires distance-relative ball hitting strength, while Holly takes more of a 'if it bounces off enough edges it should eventually go in' approach. To ensure the maximum amount of bounces, she takes a run up. More balls ended up in the parking lot than in holes, one grazed my forehead as it went past and left a friction burn. On one hole, a par 3, Holly scored 28 and there was a line of about twenty people waiting behind us.

"You want to tap it, not launch it."

"Yes, thank you, Tiger Woods. Do I tell you how to play?"

"There's no need. I have a fundamental grasp of physics."

"This is why golf tournaments have shushers. You're distracting me. Shush..."

hits the ball onto the roof of a nearby church

"That was close. Shushing certainly helped."

"I'm marking it down as a 3."

"That's cheating."

"Call the police, I don't give a fuck. Actually, I'll mark it down as a 2, I want a trophy and Tom is playing well."

"You know you can just buy them at the mini-golf shop, right? They're like five dollars."

"Yes, but I wouldn't have earned it."

Tom *was* playing well. Very well. He was a little too cocky about it as well. I'm fine with a bit of playful cockiness - maybe a fun little wobble of the head with a smirk - but actual cockiness isn't a nice look on anybody. Two or three good shots and he was now a professional mini-golf instructor and demonstrated the exact spot you should bounce the ball off for every hole.

"That wasn't where I was pointing. You were two inches to the left of the spot I showed you."

"I do apologise, Tom. That's on me. Your instructions were perfectly clear."

"You could have tapped it a bit harder as well."

"Yes, probably. I could have done a lot of things."

"Watch me... see? Straight through the crocodile's mouth... and... come on... yes! Hole in one! Did you see that?"

"Yes, good shot. Once it's in the crocodile's mouth it's pretty much a given though. There's a pipe that runs straight to the hole."

"It's called a golden eagle when you get it in one shot."

"I don't think it is."

"Yes, it is. Two shots is a silver eagle."

"And three shots is a bronze eagle?"

"No, that's just called three shots."

"I'm pretty sure the eagle thing has something to do with being under par. A hole in one is called an ace."

"No, that's cards."

Holly's mother didn't play but she watched us from outside the fence - following it around as we advanced from hole to hole. Sometimes the fence was close enough for Maria to take a sip of Pepsi from Tom's propane tank...

I should probably explain that: Tom has a really big insulated plastic mug that he takes everywhere he goes. It's about the size and shape of a propane tank - which is why I call it Tom's propane tank - and has the words *NASCAR Racing* emblazoned across it in a rather upsetting typeface. There are way too many colours and it has a chequered flag bit and I hate it. I should actually find a photo of it instead of attempting to explain how dreadful it is...

Okay, you've gotten off lightly because the colours aren't shown. There's a lot more neon than you think. Tom doesn't like it when I refer to his mug as the propane tank, but it's not quite enough of an insult for him to call me out about it, so I try to include it in every conversation.

"Another golden eagle! The trick is to bounce the ball off the giraffe's knee."

"Well done. Don't forget your propane tank."

"There's no need to remind me every hole, I'm not going to forget it. I have to put it down when I'm taking a shot, I don't have four arms."

"Three arms would probably do."

"No it wouldn't, I can't hold onto the handle and flip the straw cap open to take a sip with one hand. I'd need four."

"Unless you waited until after the shot before taking a sip. Or used your teeth to flip the cap open if there's a mid-swing hydration emergency."

"And leave teeth marks in the plastic? Do you know how long I've had this mug?"

"Twelve minutes?"

"No. What? I bought it in 1998 at a gas station."

"It's certainly well made then. Plus it's stood the test of time design-wise."

"It's practically indestructible. I could drop it off a cliff."

"You should."

The reason Maria stood outside the fence - rather than joining us on the course regardless of whether she played or not - was that it was a non-smoking establishment. The term 'chainsmoking' is inadequate when it comes to Maria as it infers a sequence rather than a continuation. Activities are based around her need to always have a lit cigarette in her hand, so most activities are avoided. She's happiest sitting in her garage with the roller-door up, occasionally venturing outside to look at the neighbour's gravel or inside to admonish Tom for something she imagined him doing forty years earlier.

"I know you tried to poison me with pickle juice, Tom."

"What?"

"Pickle juice has a very distinctive taste."

"I have no idea what you're talking about and pickle juice isn't poisonous."

"That's hardly the point. You brought me a glass of water because I was having a coughing fit and I remember taking a sip and thinking, 'Hmm, this water is a bit pickley.'"

"When?"

"1984. We were watching *Webster*. It was the episode where he had to have his tonsils taken out."

It would be extremely easy for Tom to poison Maria these days, as there's no way she has any taste buds left. I saw her tongue once, when she was eating an icecream, and it looked like a portobello mushroom.

Yes, it's hypocritical to criticize Maria's smoking, as I'm also a smoker, but I'm other things as well. You can't *just* be a smoker. Besides, awareness of hypocrisy makes it 75% less hypocritical. That's not an actual statistic, but it has to be somewhere around there.

It's impossible not to be hypocritical; everyone's annoying regardless of how annoying you are. People who live in glass houses shouldn't throw stones? Give me a catapult. One of those big wooden ones with wheels. Nobody lives in a house made of glass anyway. I've seen houses with a lot of glass, but they have wooden and metal bits as well - I doubt you can even buy glass gutters. Also, you'd basically be incinerated during summer. I once lived in an apartment that had a skylight in the bedroom and that was bad enough. It wasn't the type with a cylindrical tube going down through the roof, it was just a weird plastic dome in the ceiling that concentrated the light into a one-inch death-ray. Bedsheets smouldered, carpet melted, an unopened can of tennis balls exploded. It was more of a pop than an explosion actually, but I was just a few feet away soldering a dipswitch onto a Macintosh IIfx motherboard, which requires a steady hand. If you lived in a house made entirely of glass, there'd be nowhere to keep your cans of tennis balls.

From the earlier dialogue about crocodile mouths and giraffe knees, you've probably deduced that the mini-golf course had a theme. Most of the theme made sense - you'd definitely have crocodiles and giraffes in the same environment - but there was also a bear which was a bit out of place. The name of the establishment was Professor Hacker's Lost Treasure Golf and Raceway, so I guess the theme was open to interpretation.

The raceway bit in the name referred to a go-kart track next door to the mini-golf. It was a large track, with bridges and tunnels, and looked more fun than mini-golfing. I'd suggested, when we arrived, that we should go on the go-karts instead of golfing, but Tom gave me a look like I'd suggested we kiss, so I dropped it.

"You're up, David. Last hole. You want to bounce the ball off the third stripe on the tiger's tail."
"I'm pretty sure that's a bear, Tom."
"Bear's don't have stripes."
"That one does. They've painted stripes on it but you can tell it's a bear."
"The sign says, 'No climbing on the tiger'."
"Yes, but it's bear-shaped. Tigers are less beefy and have a longer tail. That just has a nub."

"It has fangs."

"So do snakes."

"Snakes don't have legs."

"Good thing too, otherwise people might mistake them for tigers."

"Just play the shot. What's your tally?"

"I have no idea. I ditched my tally sheet ages ago."

"What? Why?"

"I didn't see the point."

"The tallies *are* the point."

"Maybe if they're remotely credible, but Holly has cheated on every hole."

"No I haven't."

"Yes you have, Holly. What did you mark down for the last hole?"

"Two."

"We all know it wasn't two. You threw your putter into the pond after failing to hit the ball through a six-foot-wide cave entrance fourteen times."

"You said *every* hole. I didn't cheat on hole three."

"Lets just say you're the winner, Tom. I mean, we were pretty close but you may have been ahead by a couple of golden eagles."

"A couple? I've been on or under par for every hole."

"I guess it comes down to this last hole then."

"No, it doesn't. It's all the holes."

"Winner of this hole takes all."

"All of what?"

"I don't know - if you win, I'll buy you a trophy with your name on it. If I win, we go on the go-karts."

"Done."

I could stretch this out with an exciting tap-by-tap account of the shots taken on the last hole, but there's only so much excitement possible with mini-golf. On an excitement level ranging from skydiving to Tom's story about how he came by his Nascar mug, mini-golf barely rates a 3. Even real golf barely rates a 3, though it may depend on who you are playing with. I've only ever played real golf once and that was with my friend JM and his geriatric golfing buddies. One of them, a guy named Chuck, collects civil war uniform buttons.

"And do you know what this is?"

"Another button?"

"It's the pocket button off a confederate officer's dress uniform, circa 1862. You can identify the year by the ridges on the perimeter. Buttons manufactured after March 1863 were stamped without the ridges. Buttons manufactured before 1862 also had ridges, but the spacing between the ridges is slightly wider. And do you know what this is?"

"Another button?"

The last hole of the mini-golf course had clearly been designed so that every player ended the game on a positive note; it was a straight shot through a hole in a treasure chest brimming with doubloons and jewels. I didn't put much thought into my putt, there wasn't any need. The ball went through the treasure chest, along a short alley, and into a wide funnel leading directly to the hole. It was my first golden eagle and the first time I got to do the fun little wobble of the head with a smirk thing. Holly also achieved her first golden eagle, so blamed the putter in the pond for her earlier difficulties. Apparently the tape on the handle had been a little bit frayed. Also, it was slightly shorter than mine so really she deserved a trophy for all the unfair disadvantages she'd had to suffer.

Tom cleared the green of microscopic debris and crouched down, holding out his putter and squinting down it like he was playing for a green jacket and a Lexus. He took a couple of test swings, licked a finger and held it up to the breeze, then chipped his ball OVER the treasure chest.

It was a bold move that might have been impressive if the ball hadn't clipped the treasure chest's lid and bounced over the fence. Tom argued that the lid was a bit more open than it usually was, and should therefore be classed as an obstruction, while my argument was that showing off comes with risk.

"I'm not going on the go-karts."

"You have to, Tom. That was the agreement."

"Obstruction is a part of golf rules."

"It's mini-golf. Everything is an obstruction. Nobody on the PGA Tour is bouncing balls off plaster animals."

"I doubt I'd even fit in those little go-karts."

"I'm sure you'll be able to squish in."

"I have a very large head. I weighed it once and it was seventeen pounds."

"How did you weigh your head?"

"I laid on the floor and put my head on the scales."

"That wouldn't work; your neck would still have been supporting your head."

"It worked perfectly. I relaxed my neck."

"Why were you weighing your head?"

"To see how heavy it is."

"Right, but what did you need that information for?"

"I was just curious."

"Fair enough. What does the weight of your head have to do with go-karting though?"

"It's the size of my head, not the weight. I doubt they'll have a helmet that fits me."

"I'm sure they've seen heads as large as yours before. It's not optional, Tom, you went for the glory shot and it didn't pan out, so now you're a go-karter. Let's go."

"Fine."

"Don't forget your propane tank."

Holly wasn't overly keen on go-karting either. She claimed it looked "too jerky" whatever that means. She wandered off to keep Maria company behind the fence while Tom and I purchased tickets and selected our go-karts. I was wrong about them having a helmet that would fit Tom's head, but they took the padding out of an XL and made it work. Getting him into the go-kart involved a bit more squishing than I thought it would, and I had no idea how we were going to get him out, but he gave the thumbs up when asked if he was good.

There were surprisingly few people on the track. We had to wait for a family of four to finish their race, but Tom and I were the only ones on the starting line. After brief instructions not to bump into each other from a pimpled teenager with Justin Beiber hair, the lights beeped down from red to green and we took off.

Only, Tom took off a lot faster.

I'd chosen a shitty go-kart! I floored the accelerator but my top speed barely reached 25 mph, while Tom was easily doing double that. I lost sight of him on a bend and, a short time later, he lapped me. As he passed, he yelled, "Come on, slowpoke!"

It was exasperating. It had been my idea to go go-karting, so I should have had the fast one. Additionally, Tom slowed down and waited for me, *four times*, before tearing off again when I almost caught up. It was his laughter that hurt the most.

I decided a pit stop was necessary. I'd explain the situation to the Justin Beiber haircut guy and swap my go-kart for one that wasn't shit.

"What's wrong with it?"
"It's frustratingly slow. I'm being lapped by someone twice my weight."
"You don't know the cable trick?"
"The what?"
"See that metal cable that runs down the side from the pedal to the engine?"
"Yes."
"That's the accelerator cable. It's set so kids can't over-rev the engine. Just pull it with your hand when you want to go faster."

You'd probably need to be a regular go-karter to know the cable trick. It isn't knowledge you happen to pick up somewhere other than a go-karting track. For those who aren't regular go-karters but would like more information about the cable trick in case they go go-karting one day and discover their go-kart is shit, here's an illustration showing the location:

Maybe I looked like a regular go-karter to the kid who worked there - like he thought, "Here's a man who knows the track, he has racing reflexes and a steely eye," which would explain his surprise at my lack of cable-pulling knowledge. I hadn't been in a go-kart since the birthday party in 1983, and that hadn't been a good experience. I had a shitty go-kart that day as well, and nobody informed me of the cable trick. I was lapped by the other kids, over and over, and they purposely crashed into the back of me. I attempted to swap go-karts, but an employee told me to either get back in my go-kart or fuck off, so I spent the next two hours sitting inside reading *Woman's Weekly* magazines. There were also some *Karting World* magazines, but I'd lost all interest in the sport by that point.

Tom passed me again as I pulled onto the track, laughing maniacally as he disappeared around a bend. With the accelerator floored, I grabbed the cable, and pulled it hard. It was like the scenes in every *Mad Max* movie where the supercharger kicks in and makes a *phwooosh* noise. The motor roared and I was pushed back in my seat by the burst of power. I pulled the cable harder, feeling it cut into my hands, and tore out of a wide bend at what felt like light speed... to discover Tom had stopped to wait for me again.

I blamed the stacks of tires for blocking my view of the track ahead. And Tom for stopping of course. Perhaps just don't be a dickhead. There was no time to react, there was barely time to see his grin turn to terror.

For some reason my brain said, 'Not so cocky now, are you laughing boy?' instead of, 'Avoid the crash!' and I didn't even consider swerving.

"It was an accident, Tom."

"Hmm."

"Take some responsibility; it wouldn't have happened if you weren't being a dickhead. Who stops ten-feet past a bend?"

"You didn't even try to swerve."

"Yes I did. I think there was something wrong with my steering wheel. Besides, you're not meant to swerve, I could have flipped at that speed. It's like when a deer runs in front of your car. You're meant to just hit it."

"Hmm."

"They'll have you out soon. Someone's on their way with an oxy-acetylene torch."

"Where's my mug?"

"It's safe, Maria has it. Oh, did you see what Holly got me at the mini-golf shop? It's one of the little trophies with my name on it. I'm going to put it on the mantlepiece when we get home."

After a certain age, you have to start taking responsibility for your own actions. This only applies to other people, not me, as I'm owning my hypocrisy at this point, but if I had to admit it, I had time to brake. Instead, I gritted my teeth, braced, and pulled the cable as hard as I could.

I'll call it a 'momentary lapse of reason' because you can get away with anything if you call it that. Also, Tom's laughter every time he waited then drove off was way more annoying than I probably got across. I should have emphasized it more, maybe come up with a simile about an excited duck with throat cancer. Or something better. The duck one takes a bit of effort to visualize and you just end up feeling sorry for the duck.

It's not much of a defence, granted, but it's better than none. Having none would be sociopathic. Also, this was nearly ten years ago, I'm a different person now. Back then, a go-kart crash meant a few scrapes and bruises, now I have a check-list of possible injuries to evaluate any activity with, ranging from aching joints to hip replacement surgery.

Oh, you thought I meant different mentally? Like I've become a better human being? No, I just don't want to sprain anything. I bent over to get a spoon out of the dishwasher last week and had to lay on the couch with a heating pad on my back for three days. I finally watched *Rebel Moon*, mostly to see if it's as bad as everyone's making it out to be. It is. There's a scene on a dusty planet that looks like Mexico where an Indian guy flies around on a half-eagle half-horse thing. It goes on for about twenty minutes and adds nothing to the story. I almost turned it off at that point but thought, "It can only get better," but then it didn't and I was cross at myself for being so naive and watched the rest seething that I'd been tricked by the trailer into thinking there would be a lot more robots and far less flying around on things. I also watched the second Avatar movie, *Fern Gully 2*, which was better, but there were still a lot of scenes with people flying around on things. From now on, if anyone recommends a movie, I'm going to ask if anyone flies around on anything. I'm not watching it if does. I don't care what they're flying around on, I don't want to see it. I'm adding it to my movie criteria list which currently consists of the following:

1. No flying around on things.
2. Must contain robots.
3. No downhill skiing contests.
4. No magic. This includes Christmas magic.
5. No movies featuring actor Josh Gad. If Josh Gad is involved, it's only ever because there wasn't the budget to cast someone not shit. Oh, you voiced Chuck in the *Angry Birds* movie, Josh? Good for you. Must have been an absolute delight for everyone else in the recording studio. Desperation sweat has a unique smell.

I was tricked into doing a podcast interview recently and was asked, "If you were marooned on a deserted island, who's the one person you would want to be on the island with you?" It's a bit of an off-the-shelf question and I was slightly annoyed because I thought we were going to be talking about me, not someone else, so I talked about a soap dispenser I'd seen in a West Elm catalogue for twenty minutes instead. Someone with boat building skills or coconut cracking experience would probably be the best choice for a castaway companion, but if I had to play the 'pick a person' game properly, I'd choose Anne Hathaway; her sunny disposition and bright smile would make any situation seem less dire. If Anne wasn't available, I'd probably take Holly. She likes the beach. The worst person to be marooned on a deserted island with would definitely be Josh Gad.

"Yes, I get that you voiced a snowman, but do you have any skills that might prove helpful?"
"I can do a hilarious surprised look. Watch... Huuuwhat?"
"Right, I'm sorry but I'm going to have to kill you, Josh. It's nothing personal, I just can't stand you."
"Huuuwhat?"
"Okay, you wait here, I'm going to find a stick to sharpen on a rock."

It took twenty minutes to cut Tom out of his go-kart, but I think he enjoyed the attention. Sometimes when Tom is bored, or he and Maria are fighting, he will feign an illness or injury so he can go to the hospital where people will ask him how he's doing. Then he tells them about his time in the Army and where he was stationed. Also, a fracture isn't the same thing as a break, no matter who told you it is. It's just pity-whoring to state you have a broken neck when the x-ray clearly shows it's only a hairline fracture. Maybe don't stop and swivel your huge head on the racetrack if you don't want to wear the big plastic Nefertiti thing.

"We're leaving."

"Why? We have the beach house for four more days. They won't give me a refund."

"I can't rotate my head."

"Do you need to? How's your peripheral vision?"

"I'm not sitting on the beach with this collar on. I have to wear it for two weeks."

"It's not even that noticeable, Tom. If you wore a matching grey t-shirt with it, it would just look like you're shrugging."

"Thanks for ruining the vacation, David."

"That's a bit unfair. I played mini-golf."

"Benadryl the cats, Maria."

I'd argued before we drove to Emerald Isle that we should take two cars - driving anywhere with Tom and Maria is like chewing aluminum foil - but Tom was on medication following stent surgery at the time, and Maria can't drive if it's sunny, overcast, dark, or a weekday. Once, when Tom needed to be driven to the hospital after eating a sandwich too quickly, Maria saw an owl in a tree so she ordered him an Uber.

Having the cats in the car with us wasn't as big an issue as I assumed it would be. Maria crushed and mixed eight Benadryl tablets into their food before the trip and they barely moved at all. One threw up, but it did that a lot. I think his name was Bud. He's dead now. Tom and Maria took a road trip to Ohio a few months later and Bud didn't come out of his induced coma. He's buried beneath a tree on a grassy knoll behind a Burger King.

They also have cats buried behind a Wendy's in Kentucky, a Sonic in Pennsylvania, a pumpkin farm in Tennessee, and a Rest-Inn motel in Florida. The one in Florida didn't die from a drug overdose, it chewed through a bedside lamp cable and electrocuted itself while Tom and Maria were at an alligator feeding show.

The drive back was mostly uneventful, but Maria kept forgetting Tom couldn't turn his head, which provided some entertainment:

"Ooh, look, Tom!"
"How Maria? I don't have hips that swivel ninety degrees."
"It was four cows. I know you like cows."
"No I don't. When have I ever said I like cows?"
"You like the smiling one on the milk carton."
"That's a drawing."
"It's still a cow. Ooh, look, Tom!"
"Jesus Christ, Maria, I have a broken neck."
"The doctor said it's just a fracture."
"It's the same thing. What was it?"
"What was what?"
"The thing you wanted me to look at."
"The cows?"
"No, after that."
"Oh, it was more cows."

That was the last vacation we all took together. We did once go on an outing, to a reservoir to watch Holly test a kayak, but Tom pooed in some tall grass and our dog rolled in it so we left.

Mystery Monday

For years, my coworker Walter has complained that the 'bit that sticks out' on his L-shaped desk is on the wrong side. It's not a matter of rotating his desk because the bit that sticks out is shorter.

Last Thursday, while searching for a dropped pen, Walter discovered the bit that sticks out is only attached by screws and can go on either side. His discovery was pretty much up there with Penicillin, and he did a kick-punch thing as he relayed the exciting news to everyone.

On Friday, Walter brought his DeWalt drill to work, but a client had urgent changes to a brochure design and Walter had to Photoshop a black kid into the back of a speedboat instead of disassembling his desk. He considered staying back late, but decided it was more of a 'company time' thing after nobody wanted to stay back with him to help. Putting it off until Monday also meant Walter could plan his attire more accordingly and wear "proper desk-changing pants" so his knees don't get carpet burn. It's a valid concern; the carpet tiles here are some kind of asbestos/Brillo blend that smells like ozone.

This morning, primed for Project Desk, Walter discovered his DeWalt drill has vanished. He searched the entire building. Accusations were made, words were said, there was a bit of angry keyboard clacking. Most people would probably compose an email along the lines of, "Has anyone seen my Dewalt drill?" but Walter has entered full Nancy Drew mode and compiled a set of staff questions to ascertain the culprit. My favorites are Question #2: "Who fixes stuff at your house?" and Question #4: "What color are Dewalt tools?"

I asked what the point of Question #4 was, and Walter explained, "Everyone knows DeWalt tools are yellow. It's a clever trap question."

Apparently there are two clever trap questions but he won't disclose the other one. I'm guessing it's #9: "Did you take my drill? Just be honest with me, I won't be angry. I promise."

This is an ongoing investigation, so I'll update with any progress...

Not really an update, but I should probably state that I didn't take Walter's drill. I do understand Walter questioning me first though; he caught me stealing coffee beans from the office kitchen last year. I claimed I was putting the beans in a ziplock bag to keep them fresh, but he wasn't buying it, so I've had to do it every afternoon since to prove my innocence. It's become a thing; people sip their coffee and ask, "Mmm. Are these bag beans?"

According to Walter, it had to be an inside job. We have cleaners, but they only come Tuesday and Thursday nights, and the alarm log shows nobody entered the premises between 5.17pm Friday and 8.21am this morning. I suggested it may have been Professor Plum in the kitchen and Walter went all squinty and asked, "Who's Professor Plum? Is he a client?"

Apparently Walter has never played a board game in his life because he wasn't born in the "olden days" before computers were invented. He did eventually concede that he once played *Trouble* at a friend's lake house, but it was only for five minutes and he didn't enjoy it. It was too poppy...

Update 10.08am

Gary, our account manager, has a solid alibi. He wasn't at work Friday because he needed a "halfwit free day," and he was late this morning because his cat ate a stick of butter. Apparently he had to wait for the cat to poo for some reason.

Walter asked, "Did it poo out the whole stick of butter?" and Gary replied, "No, don't be stupid." Walter then explained that he didn't mean an 'intact' stick of butter, because cats are warm and it wouldn't have swallowed the stick whole anyway, and Gary told him to get out of his office…

Update 10.17am

Ben, our copywriter, is apparently a "Milwaukee Guy" and will explode if he touches a Dewalt tool. He stated Dewalt tools are just rebadged Black & Decker tools, which Walter Googled, and now they're arguing about cars. Walter's argument is that just because Lamborghini is owned by Volkswagen, that doesn't make a Mercielago a Jetta, while Ben's argument is that he once dropped a Milwaukee drill off a cliff and it actually worked better afterwards.

I was initially convinced of Ben's innocence, but he answered Question #4 with, 'Fuchsia', so technically failed one of the trap questions…

Update 10.24am

Melissa, our front desk human, also failed Question #4. She guessed, "Red?" and Ben yelled downstairs, "No, that's Milwaukee, Dewalt is yellow." Melissa exclaimed, "Ooh, I like yellow!" and Walter pounced. "Hmm, interesting," he said, "Seen anything yellow you like around here lately? Perhaps something yellow upstairs on my desk?"

I'm not sure where his line of questioning was headed - maybe he suspected Melissa of having some kind of uncontrollable urge to collect yellow things, perhaps to line her nest with. Melissa sidestepped the question by using, "Is that really how little you think of me? I thought we were friends," which effectively ended her interrogation.

Walter made a big production of crossing Melissa's name off the list but when he passed my office, he leaned in and whispered, "I'm like 90% sure it was Melissa."

Also, in case you were wondering, I refer to Melissa as our front desk human because we also have a front desk cactus.

Update 10.33am

Jodie, our senior designer, claimed she's "extremely busy", so Walter jumped straight to Question #10: "The drill was a birthday present from my dad. He's dead now." Which is more a statement than a question. I pointed this out during my interrogation, and Walter explained that Question #10 is just to gauge emotional response and he actually purchased the drill himself with Amazon points.

Jodie isn't extremely busy. Walter checked with Rebecca, our production manager, and the project Jodie is working on isn't due for another week. Nobody here does any work until four hours before deadline.

I checked the server, and Jodie's search history from this morning reveals she Googled "How to make an Origami swan" and "cute socks" and is currently looking at pictures of rabbits. I haven't informed Walter of this, as I can't risk everyone learning I can check their search history, some days it's my only source of entertainment. Last week, Gary posted a question on a forum about trailer axel weight limits, so I joined and replied, "Shut up, Gary."

Rebecca isn't a suspect as she currently works remotely from an RV. Her last Zoom call was from the parking lot of Dollywood in Tennessee...

Update 10.39am

Jodie sent Walter a text stating, "Just so you know, Melissa stole an eyeliner pen from Sephora a few years ago."

Walter has declared it "an obvious attempt to redirect suspicion," and Jodie is now the prime suspect. Walter also reminded me that Jodie came out as a lesbian last year. When I asked what that has to do with anything, he said, "Lesbians like power tools. They usually buy Makita though."

Update 10.45am

A clue has been revealed. Kate, our operations director, claims she heard a humming noise in the courtyard when she arrived. To recreate the scene, Walter made Kate stand by the front desk while he stood in the courtyard and played a Youtube video of a drill being used to see if it sounded the same to her. It didn't.

Kate isn't a suspect because she drives a white Volvo XC90. Ashley, our most recent employee, is Walter's girlfriend, so that just leaves Mike, our creative director, and he's currently in a meeting with an important client...

Update 10.49am

Walter knocked on the boardroom door, peeked in, and said, "Sorry to interrupt, Mike, I was just wondering if you've seen my drill? I think someone here took it. We might have a thief."

I asked Walter how Mike had responded, and he said, "He didn't, he just got up and closed the door in my face. Pretty rude."

It's not the first time Walter has interrupted Mike during a meeting. Once, while Mike was pitching a new range of product designs to the CEO of

Smucker's, Walter didn't even knock, he just flung open the boardroom door and asked, "Can you please tell Jodie she's not the boss of sponges?"

Update 11.03am

Mike's meeting ended a few minutes ago and he's currently yelling at Walter in the courtyard. Walter asked, "What does asinine mean? Like salty water?" and Mike did a shaky stroke dance thing. Also, Mike refused to answer any of Walter's questions and had a couple of his own, including, "Who gave you permission to take apart your desk?"

Update 11.08am

Walter is sulking in his office. Not only has he lost his drill, he's not allowed to reconfigure his desk. It's a crushing blow that has forced him to question his future with the company. I'm watching him on the server and he's looking at job listings online. We've all been there. It's double the 'fuck you' when you look for another job while you're at work. A few months back, Ben had a Zoom interview for another job *in his office with the door open* after Mike described his copy for a drinking flask product as 'fucking stupid'.

"Why would people scream after taking a sip?

"It's not 'Flip, Sip, Ahhhhhhh!', it's 'Flip, Sip, Ahh!' as in, 'Ahh, that's refreshing.'"

"Are you planning to add an asterisk to the copy explaining that?"

"No, because nobody would be stupid enough to think it's a scream. It only has two h's, not several."

"Regardless of the number of h's, every drinking flask on the market has a flip and sip spout. How does adding 'Ahh!" to the end differentiate it in any way from the other products?"

"It says, 'Ahh, that's more refreshing than other flasks."

"It's fucking stupid."

"You're fucking stupid."

Update 11.12am

...Okay, it's actually exhausting following Walter online. He has the attention span of a carrot and gave up on job listings within minutes.

He's currently watching a Youtube video about a guy who mows people's lawns for free...

Update 11.21am

A piece of the puzzle has been solved. Apparently the humming Kate heard was Mike using a handy-vac to remove dog hair from his suit before his meeting. We had a 'bring your foul animal to work' thing three years ago and there's still hair everywhere. Our copier stopped working last month and when the technician pulled out the motherboard, it looked like huge rectangular caterpillar. He said it was lucky we didn't have a fire.

It's a fairly useless piece of the puzzle, but it closes an avenue of investigation. Walter's heart isn't in it anymore so I've taken over for him. I've pretty much concluded that Jodie is the thief, but I should probably perform my own search of the premises for clues before gathering everyone in a circle to point at her...

Update 11.35am

The drill was in Walter's office behind a box of toner cartridges. Walter forgot he hid it there so nobody would steal it. Yes, it's a bit of an anti-climax, I'm not Agatha Christie.

Also, Walter emailed Mike a 'Reasons I should be allowed to change my desk' list. Reason #6 is "I'll be able to get out quicker if there's a fire," and Reason #7 is "It will take five minutes."

Mike emailed back, "Sure. Why not? Maybe knock out a wall while you're at it."

Which Walter took as permission...

Update 3.35pm

Okay, more of a followup than an update: Reason #7 was a bit optimistic. It took four hours.

It would have been quicker but the desk folded in on itself when half the screws were removed, ripping out the rest, and Walter had to drive to Lowe's to buy brackets. It was Gary's suggestion to use brackets, but apparently he meant small metal brackets, not shelving brackets. Also, a couple of the brackets have curtain rod hooks on them. Walter went with them even though it left very little leg room. There was no way he was going to go back to Lowe's, an old man made him use the self-checkout and he hates it.

I'm kind of with Walter on that one. I just want to hand over my stuff and a card and have someone else do the work. I wouldn't use the self-checkout at all if it wasn't for the fact I can get $100 worth of groceries for $12 by scanning a bag of dried red kidney beans twelve times.

"Can I check your receipt please, sir?"
"No, I left my baby in the car."

The desk is back together but it's a bit wobbly. Walter is extremely pleased with the result though - he's demonstrated several times how efficiently he can get to his door, and plans to simply avoid placing heavy items on his desk. An empty box or pen is probably fine, just not at the same time.

A Black Man Riding a Bike

"Ooh, look, Tom!"

"I can't turn my head, Maria! David broke my neck."

"Oh, I forgot."

"What was it?"

"A black man riding a bike."

"Why would I give a fuck about a black man riding a bike?"

"He looked like your friend in the army."

"What friend?"

"The black one."

"I didn't have a black friend in the army."

"Yes you did, when we were stationed in Kentucky. He bought us the mail."

"That was the mailman."

"He had a bike."

Do We Get Prep Time?

Someone I know on Facebook recently posted, "If you could go back to when you were fifteen knowing everything you know now, what would you do differently?"

First off, do we get prep time? Like are we given a couple weeks notice to memorise winning lottery numbers from the early 90s or are we just thrown back without warning? I can't think of anything that happened after 1987 that would help me without prep. Sure, investing in Bitcoin is the obvious one, but I'd have to wait twenty years for that and I'm not going to invent Bluetooth or the iPhone in the interim, because I have no idea how anything works.

"In the future, we won't need to plug in cables. Music, pictures, and text will just jump through the air to things. Also, telephones will fit in your pocket and every year the bevel will get slightly smaller."
"Sure. Did you hear George Michael was arrested for sucking dick in a public toilet yesterday?

The best I could probably come up with is the Scrub Daddy or the Fidget Spinner, and I'm not sure how I'd afford the patents or production costs. I wasn't exactly rubbing shoulders with investors at fifteen, I only had one friend and he was a 78-year-old secondhand bookstore owner. Given the opportunity to go back to when I was fifteen with my current knowledge, I'd probably pass. The eighties weren't anywhere near as fun and colourful people make them out to be, everything was brown and almost everything you did got you molested. Ride your bike to the park? Molested. Sleep at a friend's house? Molested. Lose your mum at a shopping mall? Molested.

Passing on the opportunity to be fifteen again may seem ambitionless, but not having the money or knowledge to change anything means you'd have to do a lot of the same stuff again. Nobody's going to believe you're from the future. Oh, you know the Trade Centre is going to be hit in 2001? Who are you going to tell? There was no Twitter in the eighties. And yes, I know it's called X now, but I'm not calling it that. What an absolute dickhead. Sure, fish-face hair-plug boy is enviably rich, but if I had that much money I wouldn't spend my time tweeting 69 and 420 memes to impress Reddit bros,

I'd buy Costa Rica. I've been there and it's really nice. I'd swim all day and play with sloths.

That may show a lack of aspiration, but I also don't have an insatiable need for attention and validation. To me, the best part about being 'fuck you rich' would be not caring about what other people think. The ones I do care about would be too busy swimming and playing with sloths with me to criticise my lack of aspiration.

Our lives aren't defined by any one action, it's the sum of our choices - I stole that from the new *Mission Impossible* trailer - so you'd have to be picky about the choices you made. If I were fifteen again with my current knowledge, it would be a long wait to see Holly again, and if I deviated my future too much, I wouldn't meet her at all. She'd probably be married to someone with a beard now. Someone who whittles. My offspring Seb wouldn't have been born; there's no way I'd hook up his biological mother knowing what I know now. I won't go into that but we weren't compatible; I was into design and typography and she was into penises. Mostly her coworker's penises. I wouldn't date anyone I dated, what would be the point? None of the relationships ended amicably; I was once shot with a speargun.

I'd have to make small choices if I wanted to get back to where I am, choices that benefit me in the short-term, but don't alter the long-term.

Here's five I would definitely change:

March 14th, 1989

I'd thank the bookstore owner for teaching me to play chess and giving me a job even though he only paid me in sandwiches. I'd also tell him he was my best friend. He didn't come to work the next day. I opened and closed the store for a few days until his sister came in and told me he'd died and the shop was closing. It became an adult toy and clothing store called Puss in Boots.

February 23rd, 1990

I'd have jumped into the surging river to get to the dog before it went under and didn't come back up. I don't know whose dog it was. I was scared. It was looking at me as it went under.

May 4th, 1991

I wouldn't have eaten the mushrooms Thomas Harrer told me were magic. He was a massive liar. He had no idea what magic mushrooms are meant to look like, he just drove into the Adelaide hills, jumped a fence, and picked the first mushrooms he found. They had red spots and tasted like carpet soaked in vinegar. I was on life-support for three days because my nervous system shut down. I did get high though, I had a 72-hour dream about being trapped in a spider cave. The spiders kept saying my name and when I said, "What?" they'd say, "Nothing." It was really annoying.

Thomas ate more mushrooms than I did. He actually died in the ambulance but was brought back. He wasn't the same afterwards; his movements were twitchy and he wore pyjama pants out of the house. Also, I asked him if he'd seen anything while he was dead, like a bright tunnel with Jesus at the end, and he said the only thing he remembered was riding a giant moth to the supermarket.

I was also twitchy, but only for about three months, and not as twitchy as Thomas. I could drink a glass of water without spilling it and walk without looking like a horse counting. Mostly it was just like living in a slow frame rate. Also, I was a bit healthier than Thomas to start with, he huffed a lot of whipped cream cylinders. I tried it once but it was just thirty seconds of *womp* sounds and I wet myself.

August 11, 1994

I'd have gotten out of the bath and answered the telephone when it rang. Actually, I wouldn't have gotten *in* the bath at all, I'd have driven to my friend Peter's house and hung out. I'm not sure what we would have done - maybe listen to music and smoke marijuana while he expressed how he felt about his girlfriend fucking a guy wearing a Crocodile Dundee hat. I'm unsure if it would have changed anything, but maybe, having the experience I have now, I would have thought of something to say to make him change his mind. Maybe a meaningful insight. The last thing I said to him was, "Walk it off, princess," which wasn't very helpful. It was what was written on the note he left.

Any time prior to 1997

I'd write and publish a book about a young wizard named Harry. It wouldn't need to be good, the less people who know about it the better, it would just need the characters, plot, and a provable publication date to sue J.K. Rowling in 1998 for plagiarism. I haven't read the book or seen the movie, because I don't give a fuck about magic, but I know Harry has friends named Rob and Herman and they fight a snake.

Too Many Turtles

From: Mike Campbell
Date: Monday 8 July 2024 9.49am
To: David Thorne
Subject: Turtles

David,

Can you do something about all the turtles please? There's too many. Every client that walks in says, "Wow, that's a lot a turtles."

Mike

....

From: David Thorne
Date: Monday 8 July 2024 9.57am
To: Mike Campbell
Subject: Re: Turtles

Mike,

How many turtles aren't too many turtles and what would you like me to do about them? Also, I'm fairly sure the clients say it with wonder. Everyone likes turtles.

David

....

From: Mike Campbell
Date: Monday 8 July 2024 10.04am
To: David Thorne
Subject: Re: Re: Turtles

I don't. I think they're overrated. They're just wet lizards with shells. Fish are better, we could have got ones the same color as our brand. Why am I the only one who thinks of these things around here?

It's the amount of turtles we have that's the problem, not the having turtles.

Who has 18 turtles?

It's just ridiculous. And the plastic island with the palm tree has to go, what's wrong with a nice rock?

Do something about it today please.

Mike

From: David Thorne
Date: Monday 8 July 2024 10.10am
To: Mike Campbell
Subject: Re: Re: Re: Turtles

Mike,

They're front desk turtles, not David's turtles, why is it my responsibility?

Perhaps discuss your turtle culling plans with Melissa. I'm sure she'll be delighted; she sings to them when she thinks nobody is listening and prechews their food.

David

....

From: Mike Campbell
Date: Monday 8 July 2024 10.16am
To: David Thorne
Subject: Re: Re: Re: Re: Turtles

They're your responsibility because you and Ben bought most of them.

Mike

From: David Thorne
Date: Monday 8 July 2024 10.21am
To: Mike Campbell
Subject: Re: Re: Re: Re: Re: Turtles

Mike,

The only turtles I bought are Good Looking Ben, Creative Ben, Fun to Be Around Ben, and Clean Underpants Ben. Tik and Tok are Ashley's turtles, Mister Turtle is Walter's, Swifty is Jodie's, and Flipper and Flappy are Melissa's.

Ben is responsible for the other eight turtles. He's incapable of understanding the 'attribute + name / name' joke so went for quantity over quality. One's called David Doesn't Have Any Friends.

David

....

From: Mike Campbell
Date: Monday 8 July 2024 10.25am
To: David Thorne
Subject: Re: Re: Re: Re: Re: Re: Turtles

I don't give a fuck whose turtles they are, there's way too many.

I have a meeting at Carlyle's at 11 and then lunch with Patrick. I'll back around 2.30.

Sort it out before then please.

Mike

....

From: David Thorne
Date: Monday 8 July 2024 10.28am
To: Mike Campbell
Subject: Re: Re: Re: Re: Re: Re: Re: Turtles

Fine. I'll talk to Melissa. They do look a little crowded.

....

From: Mike Campbell
Date: Monday 8 July 2024 10.32am
To: David Thorne
Subject: Re: Re: Re: Re: Re: Re: Re: Re: Turtles

Thank you.

From: David Thorne
Date: Monday 8 July 2024 10.57am
To: Melissa Woodcock
Subject: Turtle density

Melissa,

Mike is concerned the turtles are crowded in their tiny aquarium. He would like something done about it today.

Do you have any suggestions?

David

....

From: Melissa Woodcock
Date: Monday 8 July 2024 11.02am
To: David Thorne
Subject: Re: Turtle density

We could get them a bigger aquarium. They'd like that.

Will you drive me to Petco?

From: David Thorne
Date: Monday 8 July 2024 11.05am
To: Melissa Woodcock
Subject: Re: Re: Turtle density

Sure.

....

From: Mike Campbell
Date: Monday 8 July 2024 2.46pm
To: David Thorne
Subject: Is this a joke?

Did you tell Melissa to buy a bigger tank?

Mike

....

From: David Thorne
Date: Monday 8 July 2024 2.49pm
To: Mike Campbell
Subject: Re: Is this a joke?

No, it was her idea.

That Pumpkin

"Ooh, look, Tom!"

"Oh my god, Maria! I can't turn my head!"

"It was pumpkins."

"Why would I want to look at pumpkins?"

"There were a lot of them."

"So?"

"You don't see that many pumpkins every day. Must have been a pumpkin farm."

"Yes, probably."

"Remember when we saw that really big pumpkin in Gatlinburg?"

"No."

"Yes you do. I took a photo of you standing next to it."

"Oh, *that* pumpkin."

Interpersonal Conflict Resolution

The agency I work for advertised for a junior designer recently. We held interviews over the last two days, and I sat in on them with Kate, our HR / operations director, as Mike is out of the office for the next two weeks. If anyone asks where Mike is, we're meant to say he's in Massachusetts meeting with the CEO of Bose, but he's actually at home recovering after an operation. It's nothing major, he ordered Jude Law's nose and had it attached a few days ago. When the bandages come off, he will be a beautiful butterfly.

The problem with HR people is that they can't just ask, "Are you a bit of a dickhead who we will regret hiring?" They have to ask stupid questions about emotional attributes, team dynamics, communication styles, and interpersonal conflict resolution.

Here are the top ten applicant responses to Kate asking, "Give an example of a conflict in your previous position and how you dealt with it."

1. "A guy named Geoff punched another guy named Stuart, because Stuart squirted a bottle of soy sauce at him and it got on his shorts, and I broke up the fight. It was in a warehouse."

2. "I worked with a lot of women so there were always conflicts. I just ignored everyone."

3. "The manager at my last job was a massive bitch. She only had her job because she was related to the owner. I think she was his niece. That's the reason I left. And because she accused me of stealing a laptop."

4. "My coworker got really upset because a client said her logo looked like broccoli and I calmed her down and helped her fix it to make it look less like broccoli."

5. "There was a girl named Christine at my last job who was really mean to me for no reason so I told the manager she was rude to a client and she was fired. She works at Macy's now. In the kitchen appliance department."

6. "It's all about explaining calmly why they're wrong."

7. "I'm 6'5" and work out. Who's gonna start something with me? I also dig a lot of holes. My dad owns a fence company."

8. "A coworker wore a lot of patchouli and I'm hyper-sensitive to smells so we discussed it and she switched to rosewood. I'm also allergic to seafood so she ate fish outside."

9. "I just meditate when someone yells at me."

10. "The creative director rolled one of those big water bottles down the stairs at me and broke my collarbone. I could have sued the company but I didn't. I probably should have; I still can't lift heavy shopping bags or raise my arm higher than this..."

Writer's Block

I watched a movie last night about a guy who was meant to be writing a book but had writer's block. Holly chose the movie, so I can't remember the title or who was in it, but there was a duck pond on the property so he must have been a successful author. Properties with duck ponds aren't cheap. At one point during the movie, the guy's agent calls him to ask why they haven't received the first draft of the book yet, and the guy says he's almost finished and just needs another few days. Which is a lie because all he has written - using a typewriter for some reason - are the words 'Chapter One' and a single paragraph about an old man sitting in a boat.

If the guy had been married to Holly, she would have told him, "Why don't you just write ten pages per day? That way you'll have 300 pages in 30 days." Which isn't how it works and the guy would be bewildered by such a stupid statement and head outside to do some yardwork and maybe build a small jetty for his duck pond.

Friday's Intellectual Office Discourse Coincidentally Mentioning Go-Karts

Two of my coworkers, Ben and Walter, are currently arguing which of them would win in a fight. Walter is younger and rides a bicycle, while Ben once took a Taekwondo lesson. Ben stated that he carried a king-sized mattress up a flight of stairs by himself last Sunday, and Walter countered that he used to race go-karts. Ben asked what that has to with anything, and Walter explained that he has "racing reflexes" and did a quick jerky thing that looked a bit like someone with Parkinson's going in for a hug.

'Go-karting doesn't translate to fighting, Walter, it's just sitting. I've had training."
"Please, you went to one lesson and gave up because you couldn't sit cross-legged."
"That's not what happened. The classes were cancelled because the sabom was touching kids."
"What's a sabom?"
"It means instructor in Taekwondonese."

An arm wrestle was suggested but discounted as it would only demonstrate limb strength, not fighting prowess, so boxing gloves have been ordered on Amazon. The match is scheduled for Monday lunch break in the courtyard. Padded Hulk hands were cheaper than actual boxing gloves, so I ordered them instead.

I'll update with results, but it's pretty much a given that Ben is going to get hurt. Walter was born with zero self-preservation instincts and chimpanzee arms, while Ben once had to lay on a restaurant floor for several minutes after discovering bacon bits in his salad...

Update - Friday 2.17pm

Kate, our HR director, has vetoed the boxing match. Ben and Walter are going to have a Gladiator-style swim noodle battle while balancing on Home Depot buckets instead.

We actually have 36 Home Depot buckets stacked in the storage room at the moment. There was a leak in the kitchen ceiling a while back and Mike sent Melissa out to buy, 'a bunch of buckets.' You have to be specific with Melissa as she's like a reverse *Rain Man*. She once ordered 500 reams of canary-yellow copier paper because she thought that was the number of individual sheets. The courier had to make several trips with a trolly and the boxes took up half of Gary's office. Gary was away at the time because he cut an ingrown hair out of his chest with a box-cutter and it became infected. To prove he wasn't lying, he emailed a photo of his seeping purple skin egg to 'all staff'.

"I'm not a paper ream amount expert, Mike."
"How much was it?"
"I don't know, I bought other things at the same time."
"Like what?"
"Office stuff."
"Is a truck on its way with fifty pallets of pens?"
"Why would I buy fifty pallets of pens?"
"Why would you buy five-hundred reams of canary yellow copier paper? Why would you even buy one?"
"I thought Canary Yellow was the brand name. Like Red Lobster."

Also, the leak in the ceiling turned out to be a broken sewage pipe in the upstairs bathroom. I had my suspicions because the liquid in the buckets had little orange bubble islands floating on the surface; kind of like unfizzed Airborne tablets. Plus a couple of days before the source was revealed, Walter held out his hand to catch a few drops, sniffed his palm, and said it smelled like Gary's office...

Update – Monday 9.15am

It's battle day! Walter arrived this morning wearing a black Adidas tracksuit with white lines down the arms and legs, looking like a giant licorice allsort. He also brought in two swim noodles.

Ben has a client meeting this morning, so couldn't wear 'active wear', and has lodged a formal protest over Walter's 'unfair mobility advantage'.

Apparently there's also an issue with the swim noodles. Ben's argument is that his yellow swim noodle has higher visibility and therefore more 'dodgeability' than Walter's black swim noodle, while Walter's stance is that Ben should have brought in his own swim noodle if he has an issue with the yellow one. He's not swapping, he chose the black swim noodle specifically because it goes with his outfit.

There's a bit of smack talk but it's not Walter's strong point; Ben stated, "Winning despite you cheating will make it all the sweeter," and Walter responded, "Right, well I was planning to go easy on you but I'm not going to now. Also, I fucked your mom."

Ben's mother died three weeks ago, we all attended the service. I wasn't planning to attend, but then I found out Ben was going to sing. I met his mother once, at another service, and she was a miserable bitch. Firstly, when I was introduced to her, she said, "Oh, you're *that* David," with heavy emphasis on *'that'* like it was being spat. It caught me by surprise, so I said, "I don't know what Ben has told you, but he's a massive liar. Also, I caught him wanking to *Lazy Town* once. It's a kid's show."

Secondly, she stated, "I pictured you very differently." I should have said, "Good for you, you salty harpy," but I stupidly asked, "Oh, how did you picture me?" and she replied, "Younger and thinner."

I was quite annoyed by this and thought of at least fifteen clever retorts over the following week, usually when I was in the shower. I considered looking up her email address on Ben's computer and sending her one of the retorts - a witty jab about her teeth - but then I decided it might be a little weird to start a fight with a coworkers mother, so I didn't. Which shows a lot of maturity on my part. Also, she had cancer.

I was a bit surprised when Ben told me his mother had died, as I thought she was already dead. That's the thing with having cancer, if you get it and then get better and then get it again, everyone's over it by then and just wants you to die. Not in a mean way, more of a 'Oh, we're doing this again?' way. If you're related, it's a lot of effort, and if you're not, it's annoying to have to hear about it.

"The cancer is back."
"Again? What's this, like the fifteenth time?"
"No, it's just the second time actually."
"Really? I guess I just assumed from all the complaining that it was more. Must be hard for everyone."
"Yes, it came as quite a shock."
"No, I meant the complaining."

Holly's father, Tom, has bum cancer. He had surgery last week to remove a small section of his colon, but complications during the operation meant they had to remove the whole thing. He's a bit cross about it.

He basically went under expecting his butthole to be out of action for a few days, and woke up to be told he won't be needing it ever again. I'm sure he's going to be an absolute pleasure to be around when he get's out of the hospital; he's always been a belligerent old fuck, now he's a belligerent old fuck with a bag of poo strapped to his side.

While a bit of anger and/or sadness is probably to be expected after a surprise-colectomy, Tom has gone more for the 'obey my every command for I am sans-colon' approach. He texted Holly at 3am last night demanding she bring him three cheeseburgers and a phone stylus. He also asked why I haven't been to visit him in the hospital yet - which is a bit rude. Like I don't have better things to do than go see his poo bag?

"Summon everyone to my bedside immediately!"
"You're not dying, Tom."
"No, but it's poo bag changing time and everyone needs to see how it's done."
"Why? It's your poo bag."
"No, it's *our* poo bag. Also, tell David to bring me a roll of electrical tape, a signed copy of *Tanks* by Richard Ogorkiewicz, four safety pins, and a photo of a bridge."

Oh, and in case you were wondering what song Ben sang at the service, it was *Mandy* by Barry Manilow. It was a slightly odd choice but apparently his mother was a huge Manilow fan; she even copied his hairstyle. I was looking forward to Ben murdering the song, as schadenfreude is my middle name, so was pretty disappointed when he turned out to be a fairly decent singer.

"I didn't know you could sing, Ben."
"There's lots of things about me you don't know."
"No, I'm pretty sure that's it."
"Is it though?"
"Yes. Also you were a bit flat in the second chorus."

Update - 10.30am

Walter intends to wear his bicycle helmet during the battle, so Ben is currently in the mock-up room constructing a helmet and chest plate out of foam-board. He also designed his own battle crest, an eagle holding crossed swim noodles. Ben is a copywriter, not a designer, and his crest looks more like a happy chicken holding chopsticks. I might actually scan it in so you can witness the astonishing level of creative skill for yourself:

"Would you like me to redraw it for you, Ben?"

"No, it's perfect."

"It looks more like a chicken than an eagle. Or maybe a crow."

"Fine, it's a crow. Crows are smarter than eagles anyway. They're more strategic."

"Also, it looks like it's singing."

"No it doesn't. It's a fighting stance. Birds spread their wings to make themselves look bigger."

"It has its beak open."

"Yes, squawking with rage."

"Or singing Al Jolson's *Mammy*."

"Wow, racist."

Apparently everyone at our agency, and everything in it, is racist at the moment. Kate sent out an email a few weeks ago about diversity hiring, so we're currently looking for a black graphic designer. Preferably trans as we already have a lesbian and a homosexual. Mike has been a homosexual since a barn experiment when he was thirteen, and Jodie recently became a lesbian after a male Tinder date stole her television and a lamp.

"How does someone steal a television *and* a lamp? He must have made two trips."
"I wouldn't know, I was asleep."
"What? Was it a sleepover date?"
"No, it was after lunch. I made chicken enchiladas and then took a nap."
"With him there? Had you met this person before?"
"No."
"So in the middle of a date, at your house, after eating enchiladas, you said, 'Excuse me for a bit, I'm going to take a nap.'"
"I just felt really tired all of a sudden."
"Ah. Maybe he drugged you. It could be his modus operandi. Did he molest you?"
"I don't think so."
"It was definitely all about the television and lamp then. Was it a nice lamp?"
"I got it from Ashley Furniture."
"So no then."

I'm perfectly fine with any color designer as long as they don't listen to music without headphones.

There's a black guy who walks down my street almost every day blaring music from his phone; sometimes he raps along to it. I've spoken to him on at least four occasions, so technically we're friends, which means I'm not racist. Granted, most of our conversations have consisted of, "Oh my god, shut the fuck up!" and, "You shut the fuck up!" but it still counts. I think his name is Yowotup as I heard him answer his phone once.

I'm not really sure why our agency isn't more diverse, or why it's suddenly an issue. It would be easier to just delete the text on our website about being a equal opportunity employer than put it into practice though; it's hard enough finding a decent graphic designer without limiting candidates to a specific color. We've only ever had one black person apply for a design position here and his entire portfolio was just drawings of fish. They were pretty good drawings, but it doesn't show a wide range of design skills. Mike told him we'd keep his number on file in case we ever get a canned tuna client.

We did have a Mexican working here a while back, so that counts as diverse. He painted the exterior and came in to ask if he could have an office chair that was next to a dumpster.

Technically, as an Australian living in the United States, I'm the least racist person at the agency. I haven't had a lifetime of interaction with black people, so I have no reason to dislike them. Sure, there's Aboriginals in Australia, but you rarely see them unless you go on an outback tour or light a cigarette in a public park. There's a statistical reason of course - only 2% of Australians are Aboriginal while 13% of Americans are black - but it's more a geographical thing. White Australians have little interest in venturing into the outback, as it's horrible, and Aboriginals only venture into cities to visit their cousins in jail.

Again, I'm allowed to make jokes like that because I had an Aboriginal friend, named Mitch, in school. He was a really fast runner, and I was alpine-white, so we became shoplifting buddies. Basically, we'd walk into Target separately and he'd *pretend* to hide items in his jacket while I *actually* hid items in mine. Target had 'store detectives' back then, people who walked around pretending to be shoppers. They might still have them, I don't shoplift anymore so my store detective spotting skills have dulled. I don't pay any attention to anyone when I'm shopping nowadays, I just want to get my stuff and get out with as little social interaction as possible.

I wouldn't be standing at the checkout if I hadn't 'found everything I was looking for' and "no, I don't have a loyalty card. Oh, hang on, yes I do." Usually I just get Instacart to deliver my groceries. Not alcohol though; if you order alcohol you have to interact with your Instacart Shopper and show them your ID instead of just watching them through the Ring camera app. It's also hit and miss with Instacart, your Instacart Shopper doesn't know how firm you like your tomatoes.

In my shoplifting prime, I could easily spot a Target store detective. Especially with Mitch in the store. They'd all step up their price comparing act a notch and use semaphore-based codes to communicate with each other: holding up a dress to get a better look at it in the light meant 'possible shoplifter in my aisle' and a pantomime tilt of the head with a neck scratch indicated a theft had taken place. Mitch and I also had a code; when I'd hidden enough items in my jacket, I'd cough loudly, and Mitch would bolt out of the store at top speed. The store detectives would chase him, and he'd stop about three-hundred feet away - confused and insulted by their accusations - while I walked out with my patented 'what's all the commotion was about. Oh, a shoplifter? Tsh Tsh. It just raises the prices for all of us' expression.

We must have put a decent dent in their inventory over six months, but then I was caught and my photo was put up in the front window with photos of other shoplifters and my mother saw it when she went to Target to buy sheets. I don't think Target is allowed to do that anymore, which is kind of a pity as it's definitely a deterrent. I never shoplifted again, the humiliation was too much. I was crying in the photo and heaps of kids at my school saw it - it was taken with a flash so my tears were really shiny.

In my defence, the guy who caught me took me into a back room, made me undress down to my underpants, and ordered me to pull them tight so he could see if there was anything hidden in them. I'm pretty sure that would be grounds for a lawsuit these days. He also took a couple of photos of me in my underpants before he took one of my face, so who knows what happened to those. They could be on the dark web somewhere - maybe in a folder titled *Young Teen Shoplifter in Battlestar Galactica Underpants*.

Shoplifting was the only thing Mitch and I had in common, so we stopped hanging around after that. Interestingly though, he went on to become the first Aboriginal contestant on the Australian version of *Who Wants to be a Millionaire?*

He didn't do well, he got an early question about cheese wrong, but his appearance gained him a spot on the Australian version of *Dancing With the Stars*. If you've only seen the American version and thought, "How are these people stars? Wait, is that the kid from the 2005 film adaption of Oliver Twist?" you may be thinking the bar couldn't get any lower, but it most definitely can. The Australian version once had a contestant whose only claim to fame was being in a butter commercial. It was a well known brand, but still. She held up a buttered slice of toast and said, "The taste buds are on the top of your tongue, so turn your bread upside down." It might be a valid scientific statement, but why would anyone care if the butter lady is a better dancer than the guy who whistled in the Cottee's Cordial commercial? Someone should make a show called *Dancing With Actual Stars from Actual Things*.

Update - 11.30am

Ben is currently in his meeting. Apparently the client isn't happy with Ben's copy for their panini press packaging and have suggested dotpoints. Ben's not a fan of dotpoints and spent two weeks coming up with, 'Ahh, just the right amount of crisp!'

"Didn't you just use *Ahh* for the flask copy, Ben?"

"That was a completely different *Ahh*. This is a delicious and perfectly cooked with just the right amount of crisp *Ahh*."

"As apposed to a that's refreshing or falling off a ladder *Ahh*."

"Exactly."

Taking advantage of Ben's absence, Walter is shoving wads of photocopier paper down his swim noodle to increase heft. I told him Ben will see the paper, so he also shoved a black spray-adhesive cap down the noodle hole to disguise his chicanery.

"That *has* added a lot of heft, Walter."

"I know, right? I added four boxes of staples as well. And a stapler. It couldn't be any hefter."

Update - 12pm: Battle Time

Minor disagreement about bucket distance placement. Walter has greater reach than Ben, so after measuring the length of each other's arms, Walter agreed to cut 3.2 inches off the end of his swim noodle...

Update - 12.18pm

Okay. Those expecting a blow by blow account of the battle are in for a let down, as it lasted less than five seconds.

On Walter's first swing, the spray-adhesive cap flew out, followed by several wads of photocopier paper and stationery supplies. It was like a really sad firework. Outraged, Ben stepped off his bucket and pushed Walter off his.

Walter is proclaiming himself the winner, as Ben was first off his bucket, while Ben has disqualified Walter for stuffing his noodle and proclaimed himself not just the winner, but the better person. Walter claimed there was nothing in the rules about stuffing your noodle, and Ben countered that if he'd known that, he would have put a broom handle in his.

I'm kind of with Ben on this, but I'm going to construct a small trophy out of the spray-adhesive cap and a foam packaging noodle to present to Walter. The rules about staying on the bucket were pretty clear and it should prolong the argument for the rest of the day...

Update - 12.50pm

The trophy didn't turn out quite as impressive as I'd envisioned, but Walter is pleased. Apparently he's only ever won a trophy once before and that was for coming second in a sack race.

The Vibrating Man

I sold a boat to a vibrating man a couple of months ago. Yes, it's an annoying opening sentence that requires a follow up explanation about how someone can vibrate, but I couldn't think of a better adjective. Also, I'm not completely convinced vibrating is an adjective. I asked Holly and she gave me a fifteen minute explanation about verbs, adverbs, and things that modify nouns, and I mentally shut down after the first minute. As a writer, I should probably know how words work, but lack of knowledge has rarely stopped me doing anything. It's why I bought the boat in the first place.

It wasn't a new boat - it had a petrified fish in one of the cupboards and more rips in the vinyl than vinyl - but it was cheap and it floated. That was all I cared about when I bought it. I wasn't aware of the maintenance required or the marina fees, I just wanted a boat. With hindsight, buying a smaller boat that could be towed to and from a lake would have been smarter, but the 24-foot cabin cruiser meant Holly and I could find a quiet cove and sleep onboard instead of renting a lake house. At least that's what I thought.

The roof was about an inch above our faces and there was no air circulation. The first and only time we slept aboard, Holly cried herself to sleep and I didn't sleep at all. I kept thinking about how I'd escape if the boat sank in the middle of the night, it would require a lot of wriggling and finding exits in the dark, and I can only hold my breath for about thirty seconds. It might be a bit longer, I haven't tested my breath-holding prowess lately because I'm not ten.

I was once a passenger in a vehicle that crashed through a barrier and into a large pond, but it wasn't like in the movies where the hero kicks out a window and swims to the surface. The pond was only about four feet deep, and more mud than water, so I didn't have to hold my breath. Also, while the mud made opening the doors impossible, I just wound a window down and climbed out onto the roof. I was pretty angry though. The driver, a guy named Andrew, drove into the lake on purpose and he had no way of knowing how shallow it was. Sorry your girlfriend had sex with her violin teacher, but why do I have to join you on your suicidal pond adventure?

I get that the balance between emotion and logic can't always be maintained, but selfishness can. If you're so sad that you need to kill yourself, fuck off somewhere alone and do it, maybe in a forest or a quarry. You don't invite someone to the cinema to see *Star Trek: Insurrection* and then drive into a pond.

"I just love her so much."

"I honestly couldn't give less of a fuck at this moment, Andrew. There's no way I can jump from here to the bank, I'm going to have to go into the mud."

"And now I don't even have a car."

"You do have a car, it's just in a pond. I really hope it's completely fucked though, like there's mud in the pistons or something. Are you hurt?"

"No."

"That's a pity. You deserve at least a four broken ribs and a punctured lung for that stunt. I've never met anyone so selfish."

"I can't live without her. What am I going to do?"

"Yes, I'm fine, thank you for asking. Bit of a bruise on my elbow and I bit my tongue when we landed, but at least I survived your murder attempt."

"I wasn't trying to murder you. I just wanted to die."

"And you thought I'd like to watch from inside the car?"

"I don't know what I thought. It was a momentary lapse of reason."

"Ah, well that's fine then. You can get away with anything if you call it that."

"Her violin teacher. Can you believe that?"

"Yes, I've heard her play and it's kind of obvious there wasn't a lot of violin teaching going on. How many lessons has she had?"

"Like twenty."

"He was probably pounding her by lesson three."

Andrew and I weren't close friends before the pond thing and we weren't any closer afterwards. I'm pretty much an Olympic level grudge holder, and I was really looking forward to seeing *Star Trek: Insurrection.* Also, I lost both of my shoes and a sock in the mud and had to catch a taxi home in my underwear because the driver wouldn't let me get in with muddy pants - he made me roll them into a ball and hold them in my lap. I left Andrew at the pond after he became stuck in the mud.

He was fine. He ended up doing the quicksand trick where you lay back with your arms spread and wiggle your legs. He also worked things out with his girlfriend and they had a baby together, because babies fix everything, but then his girlfriend gave a blowjob to a guy dressed as Gumby at a Halloween party and Andrew crashed his car again. It was into oncoming traffic this time, which supports my earlier statement about selfishness. Nobody was killed, but Andrew spent the next two years in a wheelchair complaining about stacked washer-dryer combos and thick carpets until he overdosed on oxycodon. There's probably a moral in all this but I have no idea what it is. Maybe 'always meet at the cinema' or 'avoid people named Andrew'. I've known three Andrews and they've all been sociopaths. One of them stole my wallet and used my credit card to order a couch from IKEA.

You can tell a lot about a person by their name. Like, if someone says, "Hello, I'm Miguel," there's a good chance they're Mexican. You'd probably also be able to tell by the sombrero or if they're only ten and have a moustache. Women named Louise also always have a moustache, and men named Garth always have a rape basement. That's a generalization of course, Garths sometimes live in places without a basement and have to make do with a rape closet.

Here's a quick list of my least favourite names - it's not complete as it omits Kyle and Nikki, but it covers the worst ones:

Andrew

As stated, all Andrews are sociopaths and/or thieves. I advertised a motorbike for sale once and a guy named Andrew took it for a test ride and never came back. It's possible he used a fake name, but he looked like an Andrew; he was wearing a Simpson's t-shirt and beige cargo shorts.

Rebecca

Every Rebecca I've ever known has had inverse-iceberg teeth peeking out below two-inch gums. Whenever a Rebecca smiles, it's like watching a documentary about those scary fish that live in the dark depths of the ocean. I'd rather spend a day in a Garth's rape basement than see a Rebecca having a good time.

Dan

I don't have a problem with Daniels, just Dans. At some point they've decided Dan sounds more manly or cooler than Daniel, but it doesn't; it sounds like 'pan'. I only know one Dan, who I call Pan, and he gets rather angry about it. Threaten me all you want, why would I be scared of someone named Pan?

Joanne

Is it two names or one? Nobody cares. Most Joannes have a cellular network tower in their backyard.

Ben

Every Ben I've ever met is into craft beer and listens to shit like Hootie and the Blowfish. Also, they'll invite you to a party at their place but it'll just be Ben, his brother Craig, and Ben's unemployed flatmate playing *Guitar Hero* while drinking beetroot beer.

Sean

How do you get 'shawn' out of that?

Gwyneth

It's not even a name, it's just the sound two balloons make when you rub them together.

Lynn

Up until a few months ago, I thought Lynn was a girls name; probably short for Lynnette or something equally as horrible. I've only ever met one man named Lynn and he vibrated. That's right, it's the vibrating man from the very first sentence. Lynn vibrated in the same way that a small, fearful dog vibrates when it sees a suspicious blade of grass, the sky, a cushion. It was a constant, almost audible vibration - not high pitched like a dentist's drill, more like when you're on an escalator and you hold onto the black rubber handrail. Or maybe the exact opposite; when you hold onto a black rubber escalator handrail, energy is transferred *to* your hand - you may not even realise it at first, but then your wrist begins to throb and your watch starts shaking. Lynn's vibrations sucked energy *out* of everything.

I should probably backtrack to the day before I met Lynn; the day I listed the boat for sale. I did a bit of research prior to listing it, and similar boats were priced around the 13K mark. We paid a little less than that for it in 2018, so I guess boat prices have gone up, but I didn't want it sitting for sale for weeks or months; marina fees have to paid regardless of whether you use the boat or not.

As such, I listed it on Facebook Marketplace for 9K with the following description:

1997 Regal Commodore 242
$9,000

It floats and it's 9K.

Don't ask me if you can buy it for 5K, it's 9K. Comes with a free trailer but it only has three wheels. Located at Crystal Shores Marina, Smith Mountain Lake. Maintained by Goodhue Eastlake Service.

I rarely use Facebook so don't message me 'is this still available?' If you want a boat that floats for 9K, email me at david@27bslash6.com

Edit: Please don't ask me technical questions. I have no idea how many hours the motor has on it. Probably a million. It floats and it's 9K.

I'm not sure if it was my vivid description or people just know a bargain when they see one, but I received over thirty emails within a few hours. A lot of people asked technical questions, even though I'd specifically asked them not to, but one guy just wrote, "Sold. I'll take it for 9K and drive down Saturday to sign the paperwork if that works for you."

This was on a Thursday, and Saturday did work for me. There was a bit of emailing back and forth and we agreed on a time - the marina is a two-hour drive for me but the guy lived four hours away in Baltimore.

Then Lynn emailed me...

....

From: Lynn Hurst
Date: Thursday 8 August 2024 1.52pm
To: David Thorne
Subject: Boat

I'm very interested in the Regal. Can I look at it now? I live near the marina and I'm retired so I can meet you now. I have a 1988 Sea Ray Weekender but I'm selling it and I'm very interested in your Regal. i'd like to look at it now.

Lynn

....

From: David Thorne
Date: Thursday 8 August 2024 2.03pm
To: Lynn Hurst
Subject: Re: Boat

Hello Lyn,

Thank you for your interest but I already have a buyer for the boat. Good luck with your search.

Regards, David

....

From: Lynn Hurst
Date: Thursday 8 August 2024 2.07pm
To: David Thorne
Subject: Re: Re: Boat

Why is it still listed then?

From: David Thorne
Date: Thursday 8 August 2024 2.14pm
To: Lynn Hurst
Subject: Re: Re: Re: Boat

Lynn,

My apologies, I wasn't aware of the 'Remove listings within twelve minutes of finding a buyer or Lynn will be outraged' rule. I should have been quicker.

Or you should have.

Regardless, I only listed it three hours ago and I'm not meeting the buyer until Saturday. I'll remove the listing once the boat has been officially sold.

Regards, David

....

From: Lynn Hurst
Date: Thursday 8 August 2024 2.23pm
To: David Thorne
Subject: Re: Re: Re: Re: Boat

So you haven't sold it yet you just have a maybe buyer? The maybe buyer might look at it and not want it or talk down the price.

What are you going to do then? What do you want a maybe buyer or a certainty? I will buy the boat today!

I had a stroke last month and my dachshund died last week. I'm selling my 1988 Sea Ray Weekender and need another boat. I fish mostly on the weekends mainly near Blackpoint. Can I look at it now? Where do you live? I'm can drive to the marina now and have a look at it is it in the water or racked?

Lynn

....

From: David Thorne
Date: Thursday 8 August 2024 2.32pm
To: David Thorne
Subject: Re: Re: Re: Re: Re: Boat

Hello Lynn,

You raise a valid point and a couple of odd ones. I'm sorry to hear about your stroke and dachshund, but I'm not sure what either has to do with my boat.

I can't show you the boat today; I'm a two-hour drive from Smith Mountain Lake and the marina closes at 5pm. Regardless, I have someone driving from

Baltimore to buy the boat on Saturday. I can let you know if that falls through for some reason and arrange to meet you afterwards if you like.

Regards, David

....

From: Lynn Hurst
Date: Thursday 8 August 2024 2.37pm
To: David Thorne
Subject: Re: Re: Re: Re: Re: Re: Boat

No becasue you might sell the boat to him. I will buy the boat tomorrow!

Why are you making it difficult?

It doesn't make sense to wait for a maybe buyer when yuo have a definite buyer. I have cash and can meet you tomorrow. o buy it you can tell the maybe buyer that you soldit Is it all good? Then you can just tell the maybe buyer it's sold. he'll understand and it will save him the big trip.

is plenty of notice.

From: David Thorne
Date: Thursday 8 August 2024 2.45pm
To: David Thorne
Subject: Re: Re: Re: Re: Re: Re: Re: Boat

Lynn,

Okay. If you're certain you want the boat, I could take tomorrow off work and meet you around noon with the paperwork.

Aldo, I'm not sure what you mean by "Is it all good?" It's a 27-year old boat but has been reliable for us. If you have any technical questions, you're welcome to ask the mechanics at the marina. They've serviced and maintained the boat for the last five years.

Regards, David

....

From: Lynn Hurst
Date: Thursday 8 August 2024 2.48pm
To: David Thorne
Subject: Re: Re: Re: Re: Re: Re: Re: Re: Boat

Deal! I'll See you tommorrow at 12pm. I'll be wearing a green shirt.

Lynn

Even Lynn's emails vibrated. Or reverse-vibrated. Reading back on them now, I'm not sure why I caved in so quickly to meeting him the next day; it meant two trips if he didn't buy the boat. What I think happened, is that some of Lynn's energy black hole vibrations travelled through the Internet - attached to his emails like a pdf - and drained my ability to argue through my fingertips. Kind of like in *Tron*. Actually, nothing like in *Tron*. I'm not sure why I wrote that. It's also possible I was just worn down by all the emails asking technical questions. Why would I know what the dry weight is? I'm not a boat scientist.

Lynn was already at the marina when I arrived the next day. I didn't have to search for someone in a green shirt, because he was *on the boat*. I'm pretty sure there's some kind of maritime law about having to ask permission to board someone else's boat - maybe it's just not enforced or maybe Lynn felt that it was his boat already as we had an agreement. Regardless, he'd had a good poke around and had even spoken to one of the marina mechanics.

I was going to mention maritime law, but Lynn started talking about his dead dachshund, Bean, and it felt wrong to admonish him after learning about

Bean attempting to jump from a jetty into a boat and his little legs not quite making it. Apparently there was a bit of scrambling and a *plop* and Bean didn't resurface.

"They are kind of torpedo shaped."
"What are?"
"Dachshunds. If he went in at the right angle, he could have travelled a fair distance. How deep was the water?"
"About eight feet."
"Probably got stuck in the mud then."

We took the boat out for a water test. The throttle was a little clunky and the speedo didn't work, but the boat didn't sink or catch fire.

"The throttle is a bit clunky."
"It's a 27-year-old boat. Some things are bound to be a bit clunky."
"Also, the microwave is rusty."
"Yes, I wouldn't use that. I heated ramen in it once and my chest got warm."
"Are there any other problems?"
"Not that I know of. The toilet is hard to flush and the vinyl has a few battle wounds, but, again, it's a 27-year-old boat. Oh, and the trailer only has three

wheels. One fell off, so it's a bit lopsided, but three wheels is better than two."

"I don't need a trailer, I'm keeping the boat on the lake."

"Right. Not a problem for you then."

"So how much will you take off the price without the trailer?"

I knew there was going to be an issue at that moment. Or maybe I knew when Lynn complained about the clunky throttle. It had always been clunky and I haven't driven enough boats to know that it wasn't meant to be clunky. There were other faults that he pointed out as well; a missing latch on a porthole, a loose seat hinge, a horn button that didn't work.

"I'm not taking anything off the price."

"But I don't need a trailer."

"Good for you. Give it away or sell it."

"How much is it worth?"

"I don't know. Maybe a grand or so."

"Okay, so keep it and take a thousand dollars off the price."

"That wasn't the agreement. What possible use would I have for a boat trailer without a boat?

"I don't have a use for it either."

Once a disagreement becomes circular, you can either ride it like a merry-go-round or jump off. It had been a long drive, and I had to drive back again, and Lynn's surprise ammendment to the agreement was extremely annoying. As was his pointing out faults; the fuck do I care about a loose seat hinge? We had an agreement, it's *your* loose seat hinge. It was meant to be a simple transaction. And quick. I'd been there over an hour already.

"Right, well it was an absolute pleasure meeting you, Lynn. Thank you for the dog story and good luck with your continuing boat search."
"Don't be like that. Fine, I'll take the trailer even though I don't need it. I'll have to fix it before I can sell it though. How much will a new wheel cost?"
"It still has the wheel, it just fell off. Apparently it just needs a new hub."
"And how much does a hub cost?"
"I have no idea, you would have to ask a mechanic."
"Okay, let's ask one."

I definitely said, "*you* would have to ask a mechanic" not "*we*", but for some reason I followed him towards the workshed. It should be noted that I'd already received an unhealthy dose of Lynn's negative vibration thing by this point. I knew something was off but I put it down to the heat and the drive and being disappointed that there was a negative aspect to what should have been a positive experience for both the seller and buyer. Maybe, I convinced myself, it was just a cultural thing. In Australia, once you've agreed to purchase an item for a price and arranged to meet, there's no after-agreement haggling. It's not a Turkish bazaar. A lot of things are done differently here in the United States though, and I'm fairly slow at picking things up. It's usually on purpose, there's David's way of doing things and a stupid way.

I should probably also provide a better description of Lynn than vibrating. I meant to describe him earlier, when I mentioned he was on the boat, but then I wandered off on a maritime law and torpedo dog tangent. Lynn looked *exactly* like the Monopoly man. Obviously he wasn't wearing a monocle or a tall black hat, but if you imagine the Monopoly guy having a day off work, maybe to mow the lawn or clean out gutters, that's pretty much spot on.

I know most of the mechanics at the marina as I don't do my own oil changes. I don't even know where the oil stick thing is on my car. I'm assuming it's under the hood somewhere, it seems the likely place, but the 'lack of knowledge rarely stopping me doing anything' thing stops at motors. There's too many bits. My father used to do his own work on the family car, and sometimes I'd help, but I was more of a flashlight holder than an apprentice, and replaceable with a piece of duct tape.

"Why are you shaking the light? Hold it steady."
"I am."
"No you're not. It's like a disco in here. Shine it on the alternator."
"Here?"
"Does that look like a fucking alternator to you?"
"Here?"
"That's the battery. Just hand me the duct tape and go play with your Spirograph or something."

My father had very little patience, so it's surprising I have so much. Once, after getting shocked while fixing a toaster, he placed the toaster in our driveway, backed over it with the car, then threw it like a frisbee over our back fence. It hit the neighbour's six-year-old daughter while she was standing on a pool ladder.

Lynn cornered a boat mechanic named Stephen. I saw Stephen's shoulders droop, so he must have been the mechanic Lynn had spoken to earlier.

"I have a couple more questions," Lynn declared.

"I'm actually kind of busy at the..."

"I'll make it quick then. Firstly, how much will it cost to repair the trailer?"

Stephen shrugged, "A hub will set you back around two hundred dollars. Including labor, you're probably looking at four-fifty."

"Okay. And the throttle is clunky. Is that an expensive repair?"

"The cable stretches over time; it's easy to fix, but it's not cheap. You'd probably be looking at another five-hundred dollars."

"And how much is a porthole latch?"

I had an inkling where this was headed, but I fought the inkling. There was no way he was adding up costs to argue the price down further...

"So, with the cable, hub, speedometer, latch, seat hinge, microwave, and toilet, we're looking at just under two thousand dollars?"

"Around there, yes."

Lynn looked at me. He didn't verbally state, "How could you do this to me? I had a stroke recently and my dachshund drowned last week!" but he ramped up the vibrations and telepathically conveyed it.

"No."

'You should at least go halves. I can't sell the trailer like it is and you didn't tell me about the clunky throttle."

"It's a 27-year-old boat. If nothing was clunky, I would have listed it for 13K."

"Oh, I see what's happening here. You think because I had a stroke recently and my dog drowned last week, I'm not thinking straight and I'll be easy to gaslight."

"Nobody's trying to gaslight you. We had an agreement for 9K, as is."

:"You didn't write 'as is' in the listing."

"I didn't write a lot of things. Nobody is forcing you to buy the boat, Lynn. I don't even want to sell it to you anymore. I'd rather drive back here tomorrow and sell it to the guy from Baltimore as originally planned."

"Does he intend to tow it back to Baltimore?"

"I assume so."

"On a trailer with only three wheels?"

It was an annoying but valid point. The guy from Baltimore hadn't even mentioned the trailer. The boat had made it to the lake on three wheels five years earlier, but the fourth wheel had only fallen off a few miles from the marina. How safe would a four-hour trip on three wheels be? I'm not a huge fan of towing things when they have all their wheels; I'm convinced that every time I go over a bump, the trailer hitch is going to jump off its little ball thing. It has to be something that happens, otherwise you wouldn't need the safety chains. I'd almost prefer the chains weren't attached, that way a wayward trailer would be everyone else's problem, not mine. I picture the trailer hitch coming off, nosediving into the road, and the chains ripping the back of my vehicle off.

I'm 51% sure the trailer would just be dragged - with a lot of noise and sparks and me screaming - until I found somewhere to pull over, but what if there's a pothole for the hitch to catch on? It would be like a polevault and the trailer might land on top of the car. Who even came up with the ball thing to tow things with?

"So it just rests on top of a ball?"
"No, it's held there with a tiny piece of metal."
"Seems a bit dodgy."
"It really is. That's why I added safety chains."
"To keep the hitch off the ground if the trailer comes off the ball?"
"No, to keep it attached to the vehicle while it's shaking violently and nosediving into potholes."

"And you're set on calling them 'safety chains'?"
"Yes, I was going to go with 'life-changing experience chains,' but it's a bit of a mouthful."

I asked Stephen if he thought the trailer was safe to tow a boat with, and was a little disappointed with his answer. He could see what was going on and should have lied for me. That's what friends do. We're not good friends, but I give him a nod every time I see him at the marina and I once complimented him on a shirt he was wearing. It was moisture-wicking.

Okay, thank you, Stephen. You've been very helpful. So it's $450 total to replace the hub?"
"With labor, yes."
"Fine, just fix the hub and bill me for it. You have my details in your system already."
"Will do."

That was my first mistake, or my second if you count agreeing to meet Lynn. I figured paying for the hub would be the end of discussion, it was a compromise in order for the sale to move forward. I wasn't pleased, but I also didn't want to drive down the next day and risk a repeat of the trailer discussion. With hindsight, I should have just taken $450 off the price.

"What about the clunky throttle?" Lynn asked.

There was no compromise, it had been a concession as far as Lynn was concerned. One concession down with many to go. There's little point documenting the next thirty minutes of arguing, as it was just a looping remix of the earlier arguments. Lynn also repeated his dachshund story, twice, and added a bit about not washing his pillow covers because they smell like Bean. I mean, I get it, we have a Boston terrier named Chester and I'd be devastated if anything happened to him, but at this point I was beginning to suspect Bean may have dived in on purpose.

"Okay, I'm out. Thank you for all the kibble but I just can't do this anymore."
plop

"Okay, I'm out, Lynn. I just can't do this anymore."
"Fine. I'll eat the cost of fixing the latch, microwave, speedometer, toilet, and seat hinge, if you take $500 off for the clunky throttle. Deal?"
"No."
VIBRATION LEVEL 10 "Did I mention my stroke? I had it while I was filling Bean's water bowl..."
"Okay, deal."
"Excellent. Is a check okay?"

I'm not joking about the check. I was going to write a joke about Lynn's stroke, maybe something about Bean dialling 911, but the situation was inane enough without embellishment.

"Are you almost home?"

"No, I'm sitting in the parking lot of a Truist bank in a town called Hardy."

"Hardy is in the opposite direction."

"Yes, I'm aware of that, Holly."

"The buyer didn't have the cash on him?"

"I don't have the energy to explain at the moment. It's all been sucked out of me. I'm just a husk waiting for the Monopoly man to bring me $8500 so I can escape."

"I thought you listed the boat for 9K?"

"Yes, but his dachshund drowned."

Lynn and I exchanged paperwork and an envelope of cash. It was finally over. I could leave and never have to communicate with this person again... Which is how most private sales work. Regardless of the item sold - a boat, car, or treadmill - the relationship between buyer and seller is finalised by the exchange of cash for an item.

Apparently nobody has explained this to Lynn...

This is a lengthy email chain, so grab some cheese. I was tempted to trim it to avoid repetition and improve readability, but I've left it unabridged to document the full inanity...

From: Lynn Hurst
Date: Tuesday 3 September 2024 11.04am
To: David Thorne
Subject: Call me

CALL ME ASAP!!!!!

My number is (540) 309-xxxx

....

From: Lynn Hurst
Date: Tuesday 3 September 2024 11.06am
To: David Thorne
Subject: Call me

PLEASE CALL ME NOW!!!!!!!!!
IT'S YRGENT!!!!

From: David Thorne
Date: Tuesday 3 September 2024 11.13am
To: Lynn Hurst
Subject: Re: Call me

Hello Lynn,

I'm in a presentation until 11.30 - what's the all-caps emergency?

Regards, David

....

From: Lynn Hurst
Date: Tuesday 3 September 2024 11.17am
To: David Thorne
Subject: Re: Re: Call me

Stephen says he can't fix the trailer. The hub is seized on the bearing.

What now?

WHAT DO WE DO?

From: David Thorne
Date: Tuesday 3 September 2024 11.24am
To: Lynn Hurst
Subject: Re: Re: Re: Call me

Lynn,

How is a seized hub worthy of eighteen exclamation points? I thought the boat must have exploded or something.

Just take it somewhere else.

Regards, David

....

From: Lynn Hurst
Date: Tuesday 3 September 2024 11.28am
To: David Thorne
Subject: Re: Re: Re: Re: Call me

Where?

From: David Thorne
Date: Tuesday 3 September 2024 11.32am
To: Lynn Hurst
Subject: Re: Re: Re: Re: Re: Call me

Lynn,

Are you familiar with Google? It's an online search engine. Just Google 'Google' and it should be at the top of the search results.

Regards, David

....

.

From: Lynn Hurst
Date: Tuesday 3 September 2024 11.35am
To: David Thorne
Subject: Re: Re: Re: Re: Re: Re: Call me

Is not a responsinility do.

From: David Thorne
Date: Tuesday 3 September 2024 11.44am
To: Lynn Hurst
Subject: Re: Re: Re: Re: Re: Re: Re: Call me

Lynn,

No, I guess not. Or yes.

According to Google, Heath's Tire & Lube is the closest business to you. I called to confirm they work on trailers. The address is 12334 Moneta Road.

I also called Stephen to let him know you will be collecting the trailer - he says it's fine to tow without a boat on it.

Regards, David

....

From: Lynn Hurst
Date: Tuesday 3 September 2024 11.47am
To: David Thorne
Subject: Re: Re: Re: Re: Re: Re: Re: Re: Call me

Okay

From: Lynn Hurst
Date: Friday 13 September 2024 10.18am
To: David Thorne
Subject: Heaths

PLEASE CALL URGENTLY!!!!1 ME ON
(540) 309-xxxx

Lynn

....

From: David Thorne
Date: Friday 13 September 2024 10.37am
To: Lynn Hurst
Subject: Re: Heaths

Hello Lynn,

No offence, but I'd rather keep our communication to email. Calling would give you my mobile number and I've filled my regret quota for this month.

Is this an actual four exclamation point and a 1 issue, or just another hub thing?

Regards, David

From: Lynn Hurst
Date: Friday 13 September 2024 10.43am
To: David Thorne
Subject: Re: Re: Heaths

Heath's looked at the trailer and they said the and. is going to cost $1000 to fix!!!!! They said it could the seized bearings but would be best to change the axel. To make it safe.

Seems best to just pay Heath's to fix it .Thoughts?

Lynn

....

From: David Thorne
Date: Friday 13 September 2024 10.56am
To: Lynn Hurst
Subject: Re: Re: Re: Heaths

Hello Lynn,

That's up to you, but it seems expensive. You could buy a whole trailer for that price. There's two near the lake for under $1200 on Facebook Marketplace. If I were you, I'd get another quote.

Regardless, I'll send you a cheque for $450 this week to save you needing to contact me again. All the best and I hope you enjoy the boat.

Regards, David

....

From: Lynn Hurst
Date: Friday 13 September 2024 11.03am
To: David Thorne
Subject: Re: Re: Re: Re: Heaths

No you have to pay for the trailer to be fixed. That was the agreement. Or bring me another trailer.

....

From: David Thorne
Date: Friday 13 September 2024 11.09am
To: Lynn Hurst
Subject: Re: Re: Re: Re: Re: Heaths

Hello Lynn,

Sure, I'll pop down with a second trailer straight away. Are you sure one will be enough? I'll grab two just in case.

The agreement, as you're fully aware, was for Stephen to bill me $450 for a hub replacement.

Also, I'm a little confused; you stated thirty-six times you have no need for the trailer, so why the sudden urgency to have it fixed?

Regards, David

....

From: Lynn Hurst
Date: Friday 13 September 2024 11.15am
To: David Thorne
Subject: Re: Re: Re: Re: Re: Re: Heaths

I need it now I sold my Sea Ray with the trailer. If I need to tow the Regal I don't have a trailer.

I NEED IT FIXED NOW!!!!!!

From: David Thorne
Date: Friday 13 September 2024 11.24am
To: Lynn Hurst
Subject: Re: Re: Re: Re: Re: Re: Re: Heaths

Lynn,

I checked Facebook Marketplace and it appears you still have the Sea Ray listed. Are you familiar with the 'Remove listings within twelve minutes of finding a buyer or Lynn will be outraged' rule?

Regards, David

....

From: Lynn Hurst
Date: Friday 13 September 2024 11.36am
To: David Thorne
Subject: Re: Re: Re: Re: Re: Re: Re: Re: Heaths

I sold it but I've been too busy dealing with get the trailer fixed to take it off Facebook.

Pay Heath's within 48 hours or you will be hearing from my lawer. This is your last chance to avoid attorny costs and court fees!!!!

YOUR CHOICE!!!!!!

1988 Sea Ray 268 Weekender
$6,000 ~~$7,000~~

Classic Cuddy in great shape for her age. **More...**

Bob Boater 12.04 PM

Hello, is this still available?

Lynn Hurst 12.07 PM

Yes, are you interested?

Bob Boater 12.12 PM

No, it looks like shit. Also, every time you lie, Jesus floods a basement.

Lynn Hurst 12.15 PM

It still available I'm not lying.??

Bob Boater 12.19 PM

Oh come on, Lynn. This is obviously a fake profile. My name is Bob Boater.

Lynn Hurst 12.22 PM

Blocked.

From: Lynn Hurst
Date: Friday 13 September 2024 1.04pm
To: David Thorne
Subject: clocks ticking

I don't being tricked. Not that i was they changed their mind.

Very unprofessional!!!!!!!!!!!!!!

YOU HAVE 48 48 HOURS.!!!!

And I reported you to Facebook.

....

From: David Thorne
Date: Friday 13 September 2024 1.12pm
To: Lynn Hurst
Subject: Re: clocks ticking

Lynn,

I appreciate the 200 day extension to your earlier deadline and have set a reminder for April 2nd 2025 to ignore.

As we've established you tweaked the truth regarding vessel ownership and trailer repair urgency, what's the real reason you can't take it somewhere else to get a second quote?

Regards, David

....

From: Lynn Hurst
Date: Friday 13 September 2024 1.28pm
To: David Thorne
Subject: Re: Re: clocks ticking

I SHOULDNT HAVE TO!!!! A WORKing trailer was part of the deal. Why do I have to use my time and gas? You have 48 hours to pay Heath's to fix it. You told me to take it there!!!!!!!!!!! And you lied about the throttle clunk. It's not the cable it sthe outdrive link and is going to cost $2000 to fix. I have to the toilet as well thats another $500. You knew its broken. I had to change the oil as well that cost $150 pLus you knew the trailer was trash when you brought it there years ago. So you listed it on FB knowing it had issues. All for my attorney to argue on court. Its an open and shut case.

From: David Thorne
Date: Friday 13 September 2024 1.47pm
To: Lynn Hurst
Subject: Re: Re: Re: clocks ticking

Lynn,

Well done, there's no getting anything past you. I'm actually a fully qualified boat mechanic, specialising in clunks, and knew it was an outdrive link issue the whole time.

I'm also a certified toilet technician, but that's more of a side-gig.

Luckily, you're completely covered by Virginia law which states, *"Any problems Lynn discovers after buying a boat is actually everyone else's problem."*

It's a 27-year-old boat, Lynn. Just live with the clunk like we did, it doesn't affect operation. The toilet works fine, it's just hard to pump. Are you planning to take a lot of dumps while boating? It's a discussion we should have had the day you bought the boat.

Obviously the main point of dispute is liability for the trailer repair. I agreed to be billed $450 to replace a hub, while you feel I should be accountable for issues discovered after the sale. As such, despite the fact there was no written or implied warranty, I am prepared to compromise and pay half for the additional trailer repair costs if it means never having to hear from you again. I'm developing a twitch.

$1000 minus the $450 I agreed to is $550, and half that is $275, so I will send you a check for $725.00. I trust this brings the matter to a close.

Regards, David

....

From: Lynn Hurst
Date: Friday 13 September 2024 1.55pm
To: David Thorne
Subject: Re: Re: Re: Re: clocks ticking

$725 won't cut it.

I'll just see you in court.

From: David Thorne
Date: Friday 13 September 2024 2.01pm
To: Lynn Hurst
Subject: Re: Re: Re: Re: Re: clocks ticking

Lynn,

That's certainly your prerogative. Have a good weekend.

Regards, David

....

From: Lynn Hurst
Date: Friday 13 September 2024 2.06pm
To: David Thorne
Subject: Re: Re: Re: Re: Re: Re: clocks ticking

I will I'll have an excellent weekend!!!

Pay Heath's before Monday or be prepared to come to Roanoke and defend yourself before a judge.

I'm a nice guy until someoen tries to screw me.

From: David Thorne
Date: Friday 13 September 2024 2.26pm
To: Lynn Hurst
Subject: Re: Re: Re: Re: Re: Re: Re: clocks ticking

Lynn,

Nobody's trying to screw you. Those days have long passed you by. It may partially explain your anger at the world. That and your height of course. Time and genetics can be cruel.

I have offered a compromise, despite your accusations that I purposely conned you somehow, but at this point I don't think you're looking for a solution. Maybe you're just looking for a friend. Someone to vent to, a shoulder to help bear the weight of life's unfairness and the sting of buyer's remorse.

I get it, I bought an inflatable spa on Amazon once, but at some point you have to put on your big boy pants and accept responsibility for your decisions. Sure, the boat purchase may have been a rush decision, but you ended up with a nice boat for nearly 4K below JDP value. Just enjoy it.

I will send you a check for $725 - whether you deicide to cash it or not is completely up to you.

Regards, David

From: Lynn Hurst
Date: Friday 13 September 2024 2.41pm
To: David Thorne
Subject: Re: Re: Re: Re: Re: Re: Re: Re: clocks ticking

NO why should I have to pay the rest Ive already wasted my time and gas as well. I willa ccept a check for $1600 for the trailer and my timeand gas and your lies that is MY FINAL OFFER!!! and you did try purposely con me you knew the cable wasnt just lose and you knew the toilet was broken and when I changed the oil it looked like it hadnt been changes in years. I wouldn't call that maintaninied.

....

From: David Thorne
Date: Friday 13 September 2024 2.47pm
To: Lynn Hurst
Subject: Re: Re: Re: Re: Re: Re: Re: Re: Re: clocks ticking

Lynn,

Nobody would call it that. It's not a real word.

At this point I honestly hope the boat sinks. It's certainly possible as there's a decent sized gash in the hull from when I struck a shoal at high speed. It's below the water line so you can't see it unless you take the boat out of the water. As you own two trailers, that shouldn't be a problem.

I repaired the damage as best I could with Flex-Seal, but it could probably do with another coat when you get the chance.

Have a good weekend.

Regards, David

....

From: Lynn Hurst
Date: Friday 13 September 2024 3.07pm
To: David Thorne
Subject: Re: Re: Re: Re: Re: Re: Re: Re: Re: Re: clocks ticking

IM TAKING THE BOAT OUT OF THE WATER TOMORROW IF THERES HULL DAMAGE YOU WILL BE PAYING FOR IT FIXED!!!!

From: Lynn Hurst
Date: Saturday 14 September 2024 10.48am
To: David Thorne
Subject: Liar

LIAR!! YOU HAve 24 hours to paty Heath's or send me a check for $1600 YOUR CHOICE!!!!

....

From: Lynn Hurst
Date: Monday 16 September 2024 10.19am
To: David Thorne
Subject: SEE YOU IN COURT!!!

I spoke to myattorny and he says its an open and shut case and you will lose in court!!!! He is filing a Warrant In Debt in my behalf for $2000 plus attorney fees and court costs unless I hear something before 4:00 pm today and FYI Heath's is not happy that you authorized work that you didn't pay for!!!!!!!!! May get a mechanic lein on the trailer for money owed and storage also my attorney wants to know why you said the head just was hard to pump when you knew that it wasn't working properly AND why did you say that the boat was maintained properly when you stopped oil changes 5 year ago all this is adding up. Process Server coming coming shortly!!!!!!!!!!!!!!!!

....

From: David Thorne
Date: Monday 16 September 2024 10.32am
To: Lynn Hurst
Subject: Re: SEE YOU IN COURT!!!

Good morning Lynn,

You're in fine form today. Did you have a good sleep? I'm not sure what 'authorized work' you are referring to. I simply suggested you take the trailer to Heath's after your fourteen-exclamation-point panic attack.

Regardless, if your attorney isn't an imaginary friend created to add substance to your wispy threats, you may wish to ask him/her about due diligence being on the buyer under Virgina law.

While there's nothing I'd enjoy more than spending another day on Lynn's merry-go-round of madness, I have work to do so will have to jump off here.

All the best etc.

David

From: Lynn Hurst
Date: Monday 16 September 2024 10.47am
To: David Thorne
Subject: Re: Re: SEE YOU IN COURT!!!

If you look back at the email you sent me you will see that you TOLD me, not suggested, that I take the trailer to Bealths to get it repaired any judge will agree with me. It's in writing.

So to avoid going to court and having to pay my legal fees and court costs, I will accept $1200.00.

THAT ITS MY FINAL OFFER!!!!!!!!!!!

....

From: Lynn Hurst
Date: Tuesday 17 September 2024 3.04pm
To: David Thorne
Subject: okay then

Taking that as a no.

I WiILL see you in court. Meet my attorney tomorrow.

From: Lynn Hurst
Date: Thursday 19 September 2024 11.23am
To: David Thorne
Subject: FINAL OFFER

Apparently attorneys are on high demand here right now, or you would have heard from him by now. To save you avoid going to court and having to pay my legal fees and court costs my FINAL OFFER I will accept $1000.00. The ball is in your court.

....

From: Lynn Hurst
Date: Wednesday 25 September 2024 9.41am
To: David Thorne
Subject: FINAL OFFER

After consulting with my attorny,even though his is confident we would win our case, if your offer on $725 still stands, add on the $100 I paid Heath's for their estimate so $825 and we can be done once and for all. Deal?

From: Lynn Hurst
Date: Monday 7 October 2024 1.38pm
To: David Thorne
Subject: Last offer

After further consultation with my attorny I will agree to eat the $100 I paid Heath's if you paythe $725 Deal?

....

From: David Thorne
Date: Monday 7 October 2024 1.42pm
To: Lynn Hurst
Subject: Re: Last offer

Lynn,

While I'm fairly sure I could get the amount down to $12.50 if I ignored you for another three weeks, there's little point dragging things out. It would be a waste of everyone's time and kind of petty.

Sending you a priority envelope with today's mail batch. I'm including a check for $450 to cover the hub repair, with the additional $275 in cash.

Regards, David

From: Lynn Hurst
Date: Monday 7 October 2024 1.53pm
To: David Thorne
Subject: Re: Re: Last offer

Good.

....

From: Lynn Hurst
Date: Thursday 10 October 2024 12.19pm
To: David Thorne
Subject: LIAR!!!!!!!!!!!!!

I'm cashing the check but you owe me another check for $275 or actual cash!!! WITHIN 48 HOURS

NOT MONOPLOY MONEY!!!!!!

1988 Sea Ray 268 Weekender
$6,000 ~~$7,000~~

Classic Cuddy in great shape for her age. **More...**

Tim Ewster 2.06 PM

Hello, is this still available?

Lynn Hurst 2.14 PM

Yes, are you interested?

Tim Ewster 2.21 PM

Yes. I'd like to have a look Saturday. Can we take it out? I'll have my wife and four kids with me and we'll bring some tubes and lunch. Does 11am work?

Lynn Hurst 2.33 PM

I'm not taking your familiy tubing.

Tim Ewster 2.36 PM

Wow, selfish. Fuck you boat boy.

Lynn Hurst 2.38 PM

Blocked.

1988 Sea Ray 268 Weekender

$6,000 ~~$7,000~~

Classic Cuddy in great shape for her age. **More...**

Rod Holden 4.05 PM

Hello, is this still available?

Lynn Hurst 4.17 PM

Yes, are you interested?

Rod Holden 4.21 PM

No.

Lynn Hurst 4.24 PM

why didyou ask if its available then

Rod Holden 4.27 PM

It's not for me. It's for my cousin Pete.

Lynn Hurst 4.34 PM

is he interested?

Rod Holden 4.39 PM

No.

Lynn Hurst 4.45 PM

okay

1988 Sea Ray 268 Weekender
$6,000 ~~$7,000~~

Classic Cuddy in great shape for her age. **More...**

Ken Tushdis 11.11 AM

Hello, is this still available?

Lynn Hurst 11.23 AM

Yes, are you interested?

Ken Tushdis 11.27 AM

How many bitches will fit?

Lynn Hurst 11.31 AM

i dont what you mean. its rated for 10 occupants.

Ken Tushdis 11.35 AM

That won't work. I have more bitches than that.

Lynn Hurst 11.39 AM

okay

Ken Tushdis 11.41 AM

I have eleven.

Lynn Hurst 11.44 AM

blocked

1988 Sea Ray 268 Weekender

$6,000 ~~$7,000~~

Classic Cuddy in great shape for her age. **More...**

Garth Knight 3.48 PM

Hello, is this still available?

Lynn Hurst 3.55 PM

Yes, are you interested?

Garth Knight 4.02 PM

Maybe. Does it hairpin?

Lynn Hurst 4.06 PM

whats hairpin?

Garth Knight 4.11 PM

Not much. Mostly just been hanging out in my rape basement. Thanks for asking though.

Lynn Hurst 4.16 PM

Blocked

About the Author

Step 1

Using 2 1/2" x 2 1/2" pressure-treated lumber, assemble the wall studs using the illustration below as a reference for lengths. Secure the beams to the bottom rails with 3" wood screws. Ensure the corners are 90 degrees.

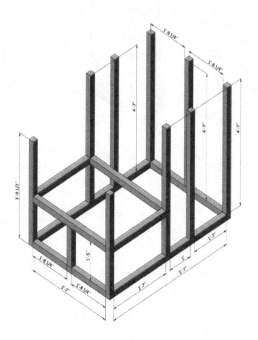

Step 2

Assemble the top section using 2 1/2" x 2 1/2" pressure-treated lumber cut to the lengths shown.

Connect the beams with 3" wood screws. Ensure the corners are 90 degrees.

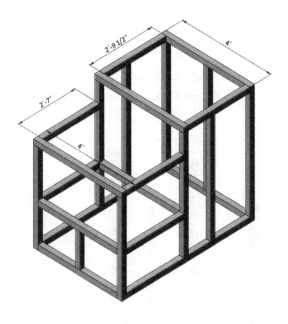

Step 3

Using 1 1/2" x 2 1/2" pressure-treated lumber, construct the back wall frame using the illustration below as a reference. You will require two boards cut to 1' 11" for the studs, one board cut to 10 1/2" for the top plate, and two boards cut to 1' for the sill and window header.

Connect the beams with 2 x 3" wood screws. Ensure the corners are 90 degrees.

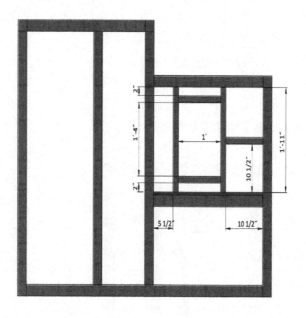

Step 4

Using 1 1/2" x 2 1/2" pressure-treated lumber, construct the left and right side wall frames using the measurements shown. Connect the beams with 3" and 5" wood screws. Ensure corners are 90 degrees.

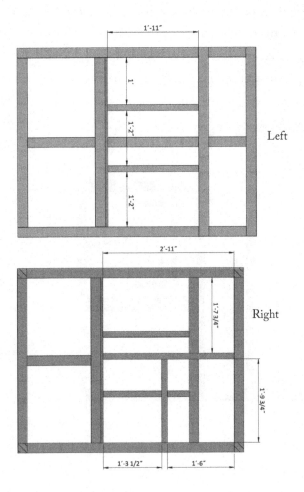

Step 5

Using 1 1/2" x 2 1/2" pressure-treated lumber, construct the front side wall frame using the lengths shown below for reference. You will require one board cut to 1' 11" for the stud, one board cut to 1' 9" for the litter tray header, and one board cut to 8 1/2" for the top plate.

Connect the beams with 3" and 5" wood screws. Ensure the corners are 90 degrees.

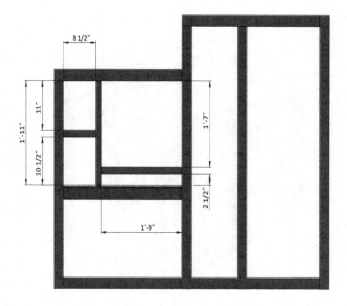

Step 6

Using 1 1/2" x 2 1/2" pressure-treated lumber, cut four rafters 2'-1/2" long and four rafters 5' long using the dimensions shown below.

Using 1 1/2" x 1 1/2" pressure-treated lumber, cut four collar ties 1'-8" long.

Using 1 1/2" x 2 1/2" pressure-treated board, cut three boards 1'-2" long for the ridge boards.

Connect the beams with 3" wood screws.

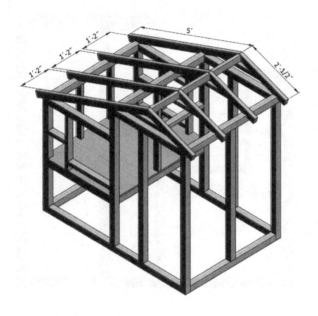

Step 7

Cut 5/8" plywood sheet for the nesting box sheathing using the illustration below as a guide.

You will require one 1' x 4' sheet for the top and two 1' x 1' sheets for the inside partitions.

Secure the plywood with 2" wood screws.

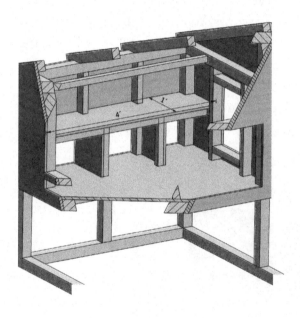

Step 8

Build the door frame using 3/4"x 2 1/2" pressure-treated lumber and secure with 5" wood screws. Cut two boards at 1'-6 3/4" for the vertical girts, two 1'-3 3/4" boards for the horizontal girts, and one board at 1'-8 3/4" for the brace. Cut a 5/8" plywood sheet to 1'-6 3/4" x 1'-8 3/4" for the door. Use 3/4" x 2 1/2" pressure-treated lumber for the door trim and fasten with 2" wood screws. You will require two boards cut to 1'-3 3/4" and two boards cut to 1'-6 3/4". For the door siding, use 1/2" x 6" boards. Assemble siding shields with 2" galvanized nails. Install two 5" door hinges (A) using 6x1" wood screws. Attach door handle (B).

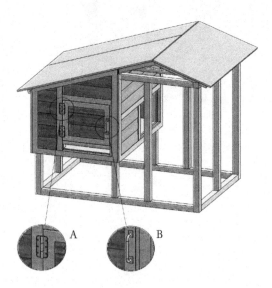

A B

Step 9

Using 1 1/2" x 1 1/2" pressure-treated lumber, construct the outer frame for the window as shown in the illustration below. You will require two boards cut to 11 1/2" for the horizontal girts and two boards cut to 1'-3 1/2" for the vertical girts. Cut recesses in each beam for splicing connection and mill a recess for the glass.

Install 9 1/4" x 1'-1 1/4" glass into inner frame groove and fasten it with window beading from four sides. Use 1/2" galvanized nails.

Insert window into wall openings and connect them with 3" wood screws.

Step 10

For the roof sheathing, you will require 34 Sq Ft of building paper and asphalt shingles.

Cover the plywood and drip edge with building paper. Install sheets with 1" overlapping edges. Use 2" nails to secure the sheets.

Install asphalt shingles using an industrial stapler.

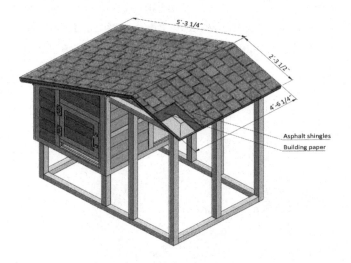

Step 11

Construct the aviary door using 1 1/2" x 1 1/2" pressure-treated lumber and secure with 5" wood screws. You will require two boards cut to 4'-6 3/4" for the vertical girts, three boards cut to 1'-3 3/4" for the horizontal girts, and two boards cut to 2'-5 3/4" for the braces.

Install three 5" door hinges using 1" wood screws. Attach an 8" door pull.

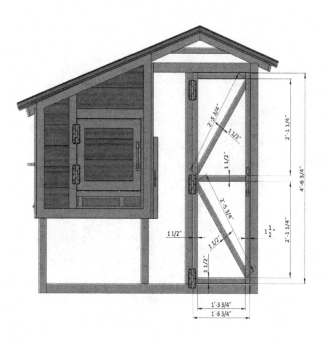

Step 12

Construct the litter tray using 3/4" x 1 1/2" and 3/4" x 2 1/2" pressure-treated lumber and 5/8" plywood. You will require two boards cut to 3'-9 1/2", one board cut to 1'-5 3/4", and one board cut to 1'-8 3/4". Assemble the frame and attach the 1'-7 1/4" x 3'-9 1/2" plywood sheet at the bottom.

Complete the tray installation by attaching a 6" door pull. Connect the beams and plywood with 2" wood screws.

Step 13

Assemble the roost using 3/4"x 2 1/2" and 1 1/2"x 1 1/2" pressure-treated lumber. You will require two boards cut to 3'-10 1/4" and four boards cut to 1'-9".

Connect the beams with 2" wood screws. Install the roost at the studs with 3" screws.

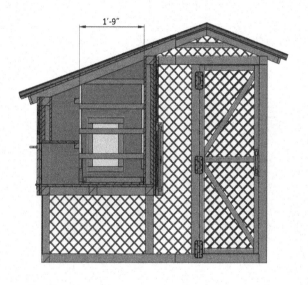

Step 14

Assemble the chicken ladder using 3/4" x 3/4", 3/4" x 1 1/2" and 3/4" x 5 1/2" pressure-treated lumber. You will need one board cut to 1', two boards cut to 3' and four boards cut to 11". Connect the beams with 2" wood screws.

Install the ladder at the studs with 2" screws.

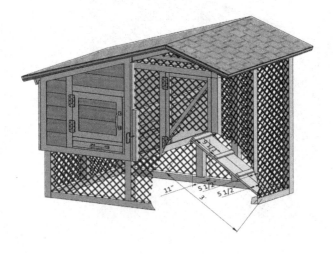

Step 15

Now that your chicken coop is complete, it is ready to add final touches and decorate it any way you choose using paint, stain, or preservative.

A solar panel is an effective way of adding a heat source and/or lighting to the interior.

Made in USA - Kendallville, IN
26384_9781735328683
12.03.2024 2007